Catch Me

If You Dare

Rainey Walker Series

Catch Me If You Dare

Coming Soon

Gotcha!

Catch Me If You Dare

L. D. Alan

Catch Me If You Dare © 2010 Linda D. Delgado

ISBN 978-0-9819770-2-7

Muslim Writers Publishing
PO Box 27362
Tempe, Arizona 85285

Cover Art by Shirley Anjum
Book Design by Leila Joiner
Editing by Debora McNichol

Printed in the United States of America

This book is dedicated to my husband – a fellow retired cop, my best friend, and my life partner.

My appreciation to Shirley Anjum for the great book cover design, Debora McNichol for skilled editing, and Leila Joiner for her, as always, professional design work.

Thanks to members of the Publisher's Forum for their expert help in polishing the text for the book cover.

Prologue

Rainey eased the seat back as the airplane's wheels lifted off the runway. In five hours she would be home. Home? The house would be empty. The last tenant moved out about a month ago and Zarinah had the place cleaned and ready for her. Rainey wasn't sure she had made the best decision, but her boss, DC Britt, had been insistent. She needed to recuperate from the gunshot wound and trauma. He insisted, as did the department shrink. Both had convinced Rainey that a new environment and time were all that was needed to heal her physical and emotional wounds.

Home? The word sounded hollow to Rainey. Grams and Grandpa would not be there to greet her. Grams passed on a year after Rainey got her degree and just a year later Grandpa died. Grandpa was just so lonely and lost without Grams. But that was a decade ago. As she thought of the grandparents who raised her, Rainey's eyelids closed and she drifted into an uneasy sleep.

The bumping of the plane's wheels on the runway caused Rainey to wake with a start. Looking at her wristwatch she could not believe she had slept through the entire flight. Rainey made a mental note to thank her boss for the first-class upgrade that made her flight so peaceful and without the usual interruptions and noise of coach.

"Enjoy your flight, Agent Walker?" the airline hostess asked, and then smiled as Rainey's response was interrupted by a huge yawn.

"Thanks for letting me sleep," she replied with a grateful smile, as she unbuckled her seatbelt, gathered her purse and briefcase, and awaited the signal to deplane.

Rainey stepped into the airport terminal. It felt so strange that no one was there to greet her. Rainey mentally shook herself. What did she expect? She had been gone for over a decade. Rainey was just one year the other side of her mid-thirties and was reminded of Sara's teasing her about being an old maid. Her best friend was single with, as she phrased it, "many prospects." She told anyone who would listen that she was going to marry a hunk from the police force who was at least a captain (she didn't intend to starve on an officer's pay) and she planned on having a set of twins of the fraternal variety, Jamie and Janie, and a nice home in the suburbs.

Rainey and Sara met eleven years before when they both signed up for a six-week archeological excavation in Mexico. Rainey was working on her PhD in anthropology and Sara was "just bumming around trying to find" herself. They hit it off right away. Their very different personalities complemented rather than detracted from the solid friendship they forged over the years.

During that fateful trip to Mexico, Sara confided in Rainey that she had applied for the NYPD. Rainey was not surprised by that or anything else that Sara sprung on her. Four years later, Sara was offered a job with the FBI, where she earned an outstanding record as an agent and finished up a Master of Criminology.

Rainey's life was planned from the first year of university. She earned a bachelor's degree in anthropology with a minor in art. Rainey thought of herself as an amateur portrait artist, though those who had seen her work held a much higher opinion of her talent. Rainey continued her education by completing graduate school, and was offered a professorship at NYU. Compared to Sara's life of guns, bad guys, and constant travel, Rainey's life was sedate and she enjoyed her books, art, and students.

Rainey's quiet existence changed when Sara convinced her boss that Rainey could help them with a witness who was too terrified to describe her assailant. The assailant was a serial killer sought in Georgia for the deaths of seven little girls ages six through eleven. The witness-victim escaped through a fluke. She was nine-years-old and had survived the brutal attack, but she would not, or could not, speak about her tormentor.

Sara convinced both her boss and Rainey that Rainey's gentle manner, soft voice, and anthropological and artistic skills were the best hope they had for getting the young girl to open up and describe the killer. Capturing the serial killer with her artist's sketch convinced Rainey to accept a position in the criminology division of the FBI. That was two years ago, and Rainey had no regrets about leaving her safe and prestigious position for the demanding and often heart-breaking work with the FBI.

Going Home

"*Salaams*, Sis Zarinah. Yes, it's me, Rainey. Yes, I'm here. I know I'm a few days early, but I got the opportunity to fly first-class so I took it, and here I am." Rainey rushed through her greeting before she had time to think. It was difficult to explain. She wanted to see her family home. She expected to be staying there for the next few weeks, but Rainey wasn't sure she was ready to face the empty house.

"Salaams, Rainey. Where are you? At the airport or waiting at the house? Girl, it is so good to hear your voice."

"I took a cab to the Phoenician restaurant in downtown Tempe. Didn't know if it was still open but had a craving for some hummus and that raspberry iced tea me and my grandma used to order every time. I thought I'd wait for you here if that's okay with you?" Rainey replied. Her words sounded strained, almost hesitant, and Zarinah picked up on this right away.

"I'll be there in twenty minutes, so save some hummus for me," Zarinah quipped, without letting on that she had recognized Rainey's anxiety.

Rainey gave a sigh of relief as she closed the cell phone. It had been so long since she had talked to or seen Grams' best friend. While waiting for Zarinah to arrive, Rainey thought about those Saturday mornings when she was a teenager and had volunteered to help pass out food at Zarinah's Farmer's Market. Zarinah had been operating a local food bank for nearly thirty years now. Amazing! Zarinah must be in her mid-seventies now, but she sounded the same as she did twenty years ago.

Rainey's grandparents left their home to Rainey…everything they owned was left to her. Once Rainey decided she would work on her master's at NYU and intern at the metro museum, Rainey asked Zarinah to manage the house and lease it to renters. Zarinah had done an excellent job, and Rainey would have had to sell the house a long time ago without her help. Zarinah was a devoted friend of Grams and a Muslim. A Muslim does her best to keep a promise, Grams had always said. Zarinah promised Rainey that she would manage the house for her and she had done just that for all these years.

"I am going to have to make a decision about the house," Rainey spoke out loud to herself. When the other diners looked at her strangely, Rainey quickly lowered her eyes and popped a bite of hummus in her mouth. *I can't expect Zarinah at her age to continue taking care of the house. She won't quit and she is just getting too old to have such a responsibility.* Rainey felt guilty as she had seldom given the house or Zarinah much thought in the past few years. She had just signed the papers and deposited the rent checks, and wrote Zarinah a monthly check. She had seldom sent a personal note or said thank you. Rainey's faced burned with embarrassment at her thoughtlessness.

The soft burr of Zarinah's electric wheelchair alerted Rainey to her arrival just seconds before she heard Zarinah's welcome. "Salaams! Salaams! Salaams! Come give me a hug, you sweet child!" Zarinah's milk chocolate face was covered in a beatific smile. Her dark brown eyes were crinkled with laughter but without lines or wrinkles…just as Rainey remembered her dear face. Zarinah was wearing one of her multi-colored *abeyas* and a matching colorful *hijab*.

"Zarinah, you haven't changed one bit…still the most beautiful Muslimah I know!" exclaimed Rainey, as she stood up to give Zarinah the bear hug she expected.

"Mmm, I see you left some hummus and flat bread for me. Ah! A lovely chicken salad. Just what I need to keep my girlish figure." Zarinah let out a belly laugh as she dug into the hummus. Zarinah was two hundred fifty pounds, given the benefit of doubt, but she was solid looking and as comforting as ever.

"Did you drive or did Mohamed bring you? I was so excited, I forgot to ask."

"No, Habibi drove me. He needed to stop in at the masjid next door, so it was no trouble at all for him to let me tag along," Zarinah said, as she wiped her generous lips with the cloth napkin.

"How careless of me not to have asked about your hubby. How is he? Is he still writing his super poems? Published any new books?" Rainey quickly said, hoping to cover her poor manners.

"That crazy old man is still carrying around that book your grandma published for him. He sells copies to each new crop of young ones and still goes to the schools to give his special talks. That lawyer friend of your grandma's, Sis Deb…the one who lives in North Carolina, is still getting books printed for him and the other authors your grandma published."

"That's amazing. What's it been—almost twenty years since some of those books have been published?" exclaimed Rainey.

"When your grandma left her business and ownership of everything to Sis Deb, some of her friends thought she hadn't made the best choice, but time has proven your grandma's wisdom," Zarinah replied.

Rainey felt a stab of regret and embarrassment. She would have known about Habibi and his book if she had opened any of those monthly sales reports. Instead, she put each envelope in a desk drawer unopened and kept telling herself each time, year after year, she would open them but never did. Rainey simply carted them in a suitcase from one town and new apartment to another.

She gave a huge sigh and placed her napkin over her now empty plate. "I am stuffed!" Zarinah patted her ample belly and agreed.

"I'll pay the bill, and then we can walk over to the masjid and see if Habibi is ready. I need to rent a car. Should have done so at the airport, but I was in such a hurry to meet with you, that I just grabbed the first cab available."

Rainey grimaced when she reached down to grab the handle of her lone suitcase, momentarily forgetting her injured right arm. "Let me get that for you," Zarinah said, swinging the suitcase onto her soft lap. "I've got a perfect carry-all for baggage," Zarinah added, without mentioning anything about Rainey's injury.

Rainey was grateful Zarinah hadn't asked questions, because she wasn't ready to talk. It had been in all the major newspapers. Rainey was sure Zarinah must have read or heard about her life and death struggle with the serial killer. She pushed these thoughts to the recesses of her mind and gave Zarinah a weak smile. "Thanks," was about all she could manage at that moment.

Rainey stood next to Zarinah at the edge of the sidewalk. They looked across the street to the mosque with its golden dome and whitewashed walls. Habibi was standing at the entrance of the large wooden double doors, talking to a friend.

Rainey's slender five-foot-nine figure towered over Zarinah and her motorized wheelchair. A sudden gust of wind blew strands of her long light-brown hair across her face. Rainey impatiently brushed the strands aside, and her emerald green eyes softened when she looked down at Zarinah, who was chatting happily away about something. *I zoned out again*, she told herself. She had been doing this since the shooting and its aftermath. Rainey shook her head to drive away those remnants of terror, if only for a short space of time. She kept telling herself it was over. She was safe. The young girl, Kinsey, was safe, and the killer wouldn't ever hurt anyone again, but Rainey still shuddered when his face invaded her thoughts at moments she was least expecting. Like now, while she looked at the mosque where her grandmother spent many hours praying during her life as a Muslim.

"You okay?' Zarinah asked, with some concern.

"Sure. I'm fine… just getting used to the bright sunshine and that unexpected dust devil," Rainey replied and patted Zarinah's shoulder.

Habibi waved to them and pointed to the blue van parked in the handicap slot. "I thought you bought a new Buick a couple of years ago."

"We swapped cars with Mohamed when he told us his wife was expecting twins." Zarinah pointed to the van with its rusted fenders and multiple dents. "That old clunker needs lots of attention, and we wanted to make sure Amel and the babies would be safe," Zarinah said, smiling up at Rainey.

"When I left home, Mohamed was attending university. Now, he is the father of two boys and expecting twins, and you are a grandma! I think I have a lot of catching up to do!" Rainey said as they made their way across the street to Zarinah's van.

As they pulled up to Rainey's house, Zarinah handed Rainey a piece of paper and the keys to the house. "The second key is to the storage shed where all your personal keepsakes are stored. If you need directions to the storage place give me a call after you get settled. The paper with the phone numbers are for the storage business, police department, fire department, the food bank where I can be found, if not at home, and Mohamed's home number." Rainey leaned across the seat and kissed Zarinah's cheek.

"Thank you so much. You were Grams' best friend and have been so good to me."

Rainey gazed at the house where she had grown up. The lawn was freshly mowed and Grams' roses were in full bloom. Rainey's eyes filled with tears as she remembered the little girl she once was, kneeling in the grass alongside Grams and weeding the rose garden.

"I had a cleaning service go over the inside of the house, and there are fresh towels and some things you might need right away. Amel and Mohamed did some shopping, but I don't know what all they bought. I told them to leave the bill on the dining room table like you requested. You can pay them after you get settled in," Zarinah said.

Rainey stood in the driveway and waved goodbye to Zarinah and Habibi. Zarinah and Rainey hadn't given the poor man much opportunity to say much more than salaams. Rainey made a mental note to thank him next time she saw him.

As Rainey approached the front door, her step quickened while a feeling of peace and tranquility seemed to spread out and reach the very tips of her fingers. *Home!* Rainey sighed, but this sigh was one of contentment and happiness. *DC was right*, Rainey thought. *It's good to come home.*

Conflicted

Rainey yawned, stretched and looked over at the travel alarm. 10:00 AM! Rainey smiled and snuggled within the deep quilt. Last night, she slept without the reccurring nightmare waking her. She felt good and rested with, *wait, was it true? Nothing to do today?* A sensation of freedom and gratitude washed over her, as she took stock in the fact that she really did need some time off from her usually busy life.

The insistent ringing of the phone registered on her consciousness, and Rainey instinctively stretched her arm to answer it. Then realizing she was not in her apartment, Rainey reluctantly got out of bed and went in search of her cell phone. She found it on the dining room table with her purse and house keys.

Rainey flipped the cover open to hear DC's smoker's voice. "Why didn't you call me yesterday? You were supposed to let me know when you arrived. I've got more important things to do than to keep track of a vacationing agent!" DC Britt announced.

"Whoa there, boss man," Rainey got in, before being rudely, as usual, interrupted.

"I want you to stop by the Phoenix PD. Ask for Major Billings. He's expecting a call or a visit from you. Go ahead and drop by as he's expecting you." DC wasn't asking. Not him. He was giving orders, and Rainey's temper began to rise.

"Good morning to you, too," Rainey responded, keeping her temper in check. "Why should I waste a perfectly good vacation day talking to some crusty old police buddy of yours? I *am* on vacation!"

"Haven't you read the papers once during the last three days? It's front page news today. No way to keep a lid on the investigation. With all your Muslim friends, I'd have thought that somebody would have said something to you, knowing you're an FBI agent. Hasn't anybody asked?" DC's gravelly voice barked back at Rainey.

Rainey felt a chill traveling slowly up her spine. She didn't want to hear anything else the boss had to say. She grabbed the scrap of paper Zarinah had given her and rubbed it across the phone's mouthpiece saying, "I think my battery is low. I'm losing the connection. Will call you later." With that said, Rainey ended the phone call. She leaned into the table and gripped the table edge with both hands. Vacation?

Rainey was no man's fool, or maybe she was. "Take a vacation and rest. Relax. Visit your friends and soak up some sunshine. It'll help speed the healing of that arm," DC had said, without batting an eyelid. His phony smile, and that's what it was, convincing Rainey to fly home for a much needed rest. It was all a ruse to get her to Arizona and back on the job.

Rainey quickly phoned Enterprise for a rental and was told a driver would pick her up in fifteen minutes. Next she rushed to the bedroom, dressed casually in slacks and tank top, grabbed the keys and her purse, and went out the front door, locking it behind her and leaving the cell phone on the dining room table. She'd get a disposable phone just as soon as she completed the paperwork for the car rental. DC could just stew for a day. Rainey was determined to have one vacation day without company business spoiling it. He would be mad, but he'd get over it. If he didn't, well, Rainey still had a gig filling in part-time for professors at several universities. She didn't need the money because she had wisely invested her grandparents' insurance money. Rainey stepped up to the curb as the Enterprise car rounded the corner and slowed to a stop.

"Morn'in," Rainey said to the young man seated behind the wheel.

"Welcome to Enterprise and Arizona," the young man said, as an infectious grin spread across his ruddy, freckled face. "Bob" began an informative monolog about the wonders of Arizona and the quality of Enterprise rental services. Rainey sat back and enjoyed his western drawl, as his words flowed over her, and the tenseness in her muscles gradually abated.

Thirty minutes later, with Zarinah's directions on the visor, Rainey was on her way to the storage facility. Rainey was determined to enjoy some happy memories while she examined her childhood keepsakes and the things her grandparents had left to her. She had avoided the past for such a long time. She didn't want to avoid it any longer. The present was not to her liking, especially after hearing from DC Britt.

Rainey's memories were mostly good ones...perhaps too good, and she missed those days and the warmth and love of her grandparents. Her loss of both of them within a year caused her such grief and loneliness...this is what she had been avoiding all these years? Today, these memories were a welcome respite from her present life and her work as an FBI agent.

"Are you okay, Miss?"

Rainey was startled by the storage owner's question. She looked at her wrist watch. Three hours had slipped by. "I'm just fine. Thanks for asking, though," Rainey smiled at the man standing in the entrance of the shed. "I'm just about finished for the day. Maybe another twenty minutes. I'll be coming back a few more times in the next few weeks," Rainey said, as she shifted her sitting position on the top of the old cedar chest.

The man tipped the brim of his ball cap and said, "Just stop by the office on your way out, so I know you're okay." With that said, he walked away and Rainey stood and stretched her cramped leg muscles.

Rainey bent over and picked up the pile of books she had taken from the cedar chest earlier. Some of the books were written by Grams many years ago, and Rainey had helped her by being her toughest nine-year-old critic. Rainey smiled thinking about their collaboration that resulted in the award-winning book series. The other books were the ones her Grams had published for other Muslim authors. Rainey smiled and thought it would be good to brush up on Muslim etiquette if she followed through with her plans to look up some of her grandma's old friends while she was here in Arizona.

Rainey found an empty plastic container and put the books inside, turned off the air conditioning and lights and secured the storage door. "Time to go and get that disposable cell phone," Rainey said out loud with a grin. She imagined DC's frustration and red face puffed up because she wasn't answering her cell phone. *So what! Serves him right*, she told herself.

Rainey stopped at a Fast 'N Go convenience store and bought a disposable cell phone. Next she drove south on Priest and made a left turn onto Broadway. There was Denny's Restaurant—the same Denny's her grandparents had taken her to when she was just a baby and all the years she was growing up. Rainey remembered the many seek 'n find puzzles she worked while waiting for their food to arrive. Grams made them to help her with her spelling, and for every word Rainey found, Grams paid her a nickel. Rainey decided to have a late lunch or early dinner at Denny's and begin reading one of the books she brought from the shed. She chose *Friends*. This was the second book Grams' had written in the *Hijabi Sisters* book series.

Two hours later, with the sun dipping behind the Estrellia

Mountain Range to the north, Rainey paid her bill and flipped open the cell phone. She dialed the number she had memorized.

"Phoenix Police Department. Major Billing's office. Sergeant Ames speaking. How may I help you?" said the brisk business-like voice of the female sergeant.

"Hello. My name is Agent Rainey Walker, FBI. Major Billings is expecting my phone call."

"Major Billings has gone for the day. Would you like to leave a phone number where you can be reached?"

Rainey grinned, satisfied. She knew the major would be gone for the day. It was after five and she knew his staff would still be hard at work and available to accept the major's telephone calls. It was on record now. She had called the Phoenix PD. He couldn't say she hadn't! Rainey gave the sergeant her call back number and wished the sergeant a pleasant evening.

Talking to herself again, something people who lived alone seemed to do frequently, Rainey supposed, she said out loud, "I probably should get a copy of the Arizona Republic and see what the boss is so excited about."

A couple walking by Rainey in the parking lot looked around to see who Rainey was talking to, and when they didn't see anyone, they grinned. Rainey noticed them out of the corner of her eye and blushed. *I've got to stop doing this*, she thought.

The morning and evening editions were sold out at another Fast 'N Go. Rainey decided to go online and read the daily paper to get a feel for what the phone call from her boss was about. As she walked through the door, the cell phone she left on the dining room table started ringing. She picked it up with a feeling of relief when she saw the call was from Zarinah. "Salaams, Zarinah."

"Salaams, Rainey. Did you have a good night's sleep and a restful day?"

"I slept soundly and spent a greater part of the day at the storage shed. Brought back some of Grams' books to read in the evenings, too." Rainey replied.

"I called because I thought you might like to go with me to the masjid tomorrow. The sisters are having their usual weekly meeting, and some of your grandma's friends you know will be there. They would love to see you, and as you have such a short time to vacation, I thought this might be helpful and save you time setting up visits. You know how we Muslims are...busy, busy, busy with family, meetings, causes, and such."

"I have something to do in the morning, but if the meeting is in the afternoon, I'd love to go." The pleasure of seeing old friends was in the warmth of her voice.

"We are meeting at two for an hour or more, depending. Will this work for you?" Zarinah asked.

"Yes it will. Do you have a scarf you can lend me? I'd rather cover my hair while being inside the masjid. I know it's not required, but you remember I always wore a hijab whenever my grandmother took me there."

"I'll bring one for you, and you can keep it with you in case you drop by for another visit while you are here."

"Thanks, Zarinah. See you tomorrow."

"As salaam'alaykum, Rainey...until tomorrow," Zarinah said and hung up.

Rainey went to the bedroom and exchanged her slacks and tank-top for some lounging pajamas and went back to the kitchen to make herself a cup of hot tea. Taking the tea and her laptop with her, she went out the back door to the patio and settled herself comfortably in Grams' porch swing. As her tea cooled enough to sip, Rainey powered up the Internet and did a search for the Arizona Republic. Within seconds, the headlines assaulted Rainey's eyes.

Third Victim of Scarf Killer Found in Home

PHOENIX, AZ - Phoenix police spokesman, Captain Martin Edgeway, in a news briefing stated "No comment" when asked if the death of Amatullah Amin was at the hands of the murderer now known as the Scarf Killer. When asked if a serial killer was operating in the Phoenix metropolitan area he again stated, "No comment." Republic reporter, Casey Brown, pressed Captain Edgeway and asked if these killings were hate crimes against Muslims and what the police department was doing to protect the Muslim female community. Again Captain Edgeway replied with "No Comment."

Rainey's eyes drifted away from the computer screen as her thoughts traveled back to three months ago when she had fought for her own life and the life of the serial killer's final victim. Rainey was working in the safe house with the young girl who had survived the killer's attack. Dubbed by the police "The Friday Stalker," the killer stalked victims for weeks and then killed and mutilated them on Fridays. Perversely, he told the police where to find the body once he was through mutilating it.

The Friday Stalker followed Rainey for weeks. He knew she would be doing the sketch of his own face by working with the nine-year-old he left for dead. He had been unable to verify the kill or deface the body because the police interrupted him, and he narrowly escaped. He searched every cemetery for the burial place of his victim, hoping to finish defiling the body. When he realized she was still alive, he had to change plans.

Knowing how police work, the killer correctly determined that his victim was being protected. He made his plan carefully and then began to stalk Rainey. Rainey Walker was a minor celebrity, having sketched the faces of several wanted criminals which aided in their capture or death. The police had become complacent. With a little work, it was easy for the killer to find the safe house. With even less work, the killer overpowered the FBI agent relaxing in a chair outside the safe house door.

But the killer made an error in judgment: he had not bargained on Rainey being armed and an expert marksman. When the killer climbed through the bedroom window with weapon and silencer drawn, he was confronted by Rainey and the young girl's piercing screams as she clung to Rainey's waist. Rainey threw the girl to the floor as she took the bullet meant for the child in her right shoulder, then drew her weapon with her left hand and fired twice in rapid succession with deadly accuracy.

The ringing of her phone brought Rainey back to the present. She shivered as she unconsciously touched the scar on her shoulder. The smell of blood and gun powder assaulted her, though she knew she was in her home in Arizona, and not in the safe house. Taking the life of someone, even a psycho like the Friday Stalker, had left a scar on her spirit greater than the one on her shoulder. Rainey was grateful that she could save the young girl's life and her own, yet she regretted having to take a life to do so.

Sara

"Rainey? Are you there? Are you okay? It's me Sara."

Rainey could hear her friend's questions and the concern in her voice as she struggled to respond. "I'm okay, Sara."

"You promised to call me once you got to Arizona and you've been there almost two days now!"

"I know. I meant to call, but DC Britt has been calling me all day about meeting some Phoenix Police official, and now I know why. I just started reading the Arizona Republic about the probability of a serial killer operating in the Phoenix area. So far, the local police are giving the usual 'no comment,' but the latest killing has all the earmarks of a serial killer. I was getting ready to read the other articles about the earlier killings when you called."

"So ya think that's why DC wants you to meet with the Phoenix PD official?"

Sara's question was more a statement than a question, and there was a funny catch in her voice. She was just too casual. Rainey's antenna went into high alert as rapidly growing suspicion about her boss and friend surfaced. Rainey did not want to believe her best friend would be part of her being dragged into a serial killer investigation, but Sara's tone of voice and that question were saying something else. Rainey's temper was on a short fuse these days and her friend was about to feel the heat.

"What do *you* know about these killings, Sara?" Rainey's voice was raised an octave higher and sugar sweet.

Sara knew better than to play clueless. It would only make Rainey angrier.

"Rainey, you know how the Bureau does things," Sara said, using her best conciliatory voice.

"Refresh my memory. Go ahead and tell me," Rainey replied with steel lacing each word.

Sara sucked in. "The Bureau was contacted about the killings in Phoenix after the second body was found using the explicit directions of the killer. That was two months ago. You were on leave, so nothing crossed your desk. You weren't in the loop. DC Britt remembered your grandmother's ties to the Muslim community in Phoenix, and somebody decided that you should go there to work with the local police department, using your past associations in the community to gather intelligence and develop some leads."

"You mean abuse the trust of my friends? Have them think I am on vacation recovering from my injury when my real purpose is to spy on them?" Rainey was close to shouting at her friend at this point.

Sara found herself getting peeved with her friend. "You are an agent with the FBI. There is a psycho serial killer loose and targeting Muslim women in your hometown community. You know some of the members in the community and they like you. They trust you. They don't trust anyone with the Phoenix PD and they sure as hell don't trust the F-B-I! You would not be deceiving your friends. You are on vacation leave and you are recuperating from a line-of-duty injury. But you are still an officer sworn to uphold the law, Rainey. Friends or not…you have a duty to try and help find this killer. And yes, if it means gathering information from people who are your friends for the sake of helping find this killer and saving lives, I just don't see what kind of problem you would have doing that!"

Sara waited as the silence from Rainey's end of the conversation continued. "I'll think about what you just said," replied Rainey stiffly. "So how do you fit into all this?"

Sara sighed deeply and then forged ahead, "I am supposed to come visit you as your best friend. I am still your best friend, aren't I?" Without waiting for Rainey to answer, Sara continued, "You would introduce me to your friends in the community so they would not feel uncomfortable talking with me."

"So do I introduce you as my best friend or as an FBI agent?" Rainey replied sarcastically.

"I'm going to hang up now, Rainey, before I lose the last of my patience. I know you're meeting with Major Billings tomorrow. After you talk to him, give me a call."

Rainey sat holding her cell phone hearing the disconnect click from the other end. *Oh boy! Sara is royally ticked off with me*, Rainey thought, as she put the phone down and turned her attention back to her computer screen. Rainey didn't want to continue reading, but she felt compelled, and when she finished, did a search for everything she could find about the killings. Next, Rainey went to the "known" e-groups and websites where members chatted about the killings and finally, using special codes and email IDs, she checked the private websites where sick people discussed and glorified their newest hero.

It was well after midnight when Rainey shut down the Internet connection. Several times while reading the sickos' trash talk, Rainey had broken into a cold sweat and had to take a time out to slow her rapid pulse. She felt it was too soon for her to become involved in another serial killer case. Sara, DC, and the powers-that-be just didn't know how she felt. They couldn't understand the deep fear that ran through her whenever she thought about the Friday Stalker. They didn't know that Rainey had not gotten her fear under control. Rainey wasn't sure if she even wanted to continue working for the Bureau. Maybe it wasn't about wanting to, as much as being emotionally and psychologically fit to continue? Rainey joined the FBI to provide anthropological services for identifying bones and skeletons and for drawing sketches of suspects, witnesses, and victims. She hadn't planned on being a field agent like Sara, who thrived on her work and embraced the dangers of the job.

Rainey picked up her department issued cell phone, clicked on Voice Mail and listened again to the voice of Sergeant Ames, "Hello Agent Walker. Sergeant Ames calling for Major Billings. He knows you are on vacation and said he would appreciate it if you could stop by tomorrow morning at your convenience. Anytime before noon is fine. Just give your name at the duty desk and I'll meet you. We look forward to seeing you tomorrow."

Rainey knew she could not avoid this meeting. She sent a text message advising Sergeant Ames she would be at the Phoenix PD at ten.

Rainey was exhausted…too tired even to take a shower. She checked the door locks, turned out the lights, and headed for her bedroom. She was sure she would have no trouble falling asleep. Wrong again!

Rainey's mind refused to stop thinking, no matter what she tried to do. At 2 AM, tossing back the bed covers, Rainey padded barefoot down the hallway, crossed the family room, out the back kitchen door, and sat down in Grams' porch swing. The desert air was slightly chilly, so she pulled the swing cover around her shoulders. She gazed at the dark sky filled with stars and a full moon which chased away any shadows in the back yard. It was harder in these familiar and comforting surroundings to think about what was in store for Rainey at the Phoenix PD in just a few hours.

Rainey dreaded the territorial gamesmanship between the FBI and Phoenix PD, which was bound to surface once Phoenix officers and detectives learned their brass had called in the FBI.

Rainey would be representing the FBI and take the brunt of the sarcasm and innuendo. The Bureau agents weren't above playing the game, either. FBI agents were generally perceived by local law enforcement agencies as arrogant, unwilling to share information, and almost universally accused of stealing the limelight and glory when a case ended successfully.

Rainey shuddered as she thought about all the administrative, political, and working landmines she'd have to navigate. Usually a higher ranking agent would be sent to coordinate the participation of the FBI, but Rainey had "special" qualifications...knowledge of Islamic practices and beliefs, as well as having personal connections in the Muslim community.

Rainey's mind drifted back to the Friday Stalker joint task force murder room where task force members worked and held briefings. Every day those horrible pictures on the Victim Board greeted the task force. Each photograph was a silent visual reminder of what they were doing and why.

Rainey replayed her conversation with Sara and felt lonely. She and Sara rarely had differences that had led to one of them hanging up on the other. Sure they had disagreements about lots of minor stuff. They were so different in their upbringing and outlook on life, yet they shared common values and beliefs that were the cement in their friendship.

Rainey trusted Sara's judgment and her truthfulness. She saw through Sara's innocent sounding questions and Sara knew Rainey knew. There wasn't much they kept secret from each other. It had been hard for Rainey to keep Sara in the dark about her feelings toward the Friday Stalker killing and doubts about her fitness. Rainey did not share this information, though, as it would compromise Sara. She would be placed in a position of either keeping Rainey's confidence or reporting a possible unfit agent to her supervisor.

Two tears traveled slowly down Rainey's cheeks. "Oh, Grams! I need your wise counsel," Rainey spoke softly into the silence surrounding her. Rainey did not share her grandmother's certain belief that all that happened was God's will. Grams had taught her about Islam by example, but Rainey had not become a Muslim. As the years went by, and her loneliness increased with the passing of her grandparents, Rainey had forgotten how to trust and how to pray.

Rainey yawned and slowly massaged her right shoulder. The cool morning air was causing it to throb. She got up from the swing and headed back into the house. Once more snuggling down in her bed, Rainey hoped that sleep would silence her thoughts and ease the ache of loneliness.

Phoenix PD

Rainey struggled to open her eyes. They were gritty from the tears she had shed a few short hours earlier. It was eight o'clock and if she hurried she'd have time for a quick jog, shower, and light breakfast before leaving for the appointment with Major Billings.

Rainey decided to jog at a park six blocks from her home. The park had an abundance of running paths and jogger trails as well as paths for cyclists, but this morning, the park was empty and quiet. Thoughts of killers and quarreling with her best friend were lost as Rainey gave herself up to the pleasure of jogging in the glorious Arizona morning. To her left, she noticed a tall woman in a bright red baseball cap jogging in the opposite direction. As they were almost in a horizontal line from each other the jogger looked over at Rainey and smiled. Rainey lifted her hand and gave the friendly jogger a wave.

A short time later, Rainey was at home in the shower when the department-issued phone began to ring. Rainey grabbed a towel and hurried to make a grab for it. When she opened the phone she got voice mail. "Hi Rainey. It's me, Sara. I told DC that the only way I was getting on a plane to Arizona is if you asked me. Love you. Call me."

Rainey's lips twitched and then spread into a grin. "God love you, Sara," Rainey murmured and replayed the mail to hear her friend's voice again. Sara's message was just what Rainey needed to be ready to meet Major Billings and the task force officers in their murder room. If Sara would put her job on the line for Rainey, then Rainey owed it to Sara and to the Muslim community to go to this meeting with an open mind and stop feeling sorry for herself. Sara was right. The next victim could be a Muslimah she knew... maybe a friend of her grandmother's. If she did nothing, could Rainey live with that? The answer was No.

Rainey replied with a text message. "On my way to Phoenix PD. Don't forget - bring my off-duty weapon. Send me flight number and arrival time. Love you too! PS - tell DC he owes me big time."

Rainey dressed carefully for this meeting. She knew every single officer, detective, secretary...anyone and everyone connected to this case would be giving her the once over and looking for something to criticize. She chose a navy 2-piece linen suit with a no-frills silk blouse. Low-heeled navy pumps and no nylons. A matching navy purse that held a pen and small notebook, a dozen or so business cards, her flat badge, key ring, her driver's license and a credit card were all she needed.

As she was headed out the door she backtracked, picked up her briefcase, and dumped the contents on the table. She carried the empty briefcase in her left hand, with her purse slung down from her shoulder from a medium strap. She felt half dressed. Her Bureau-issued Glock was in her locker back at headquarters, so there was no need for a shoulder or ankle holster, and the break-away compartment of her briefcase was empty. She hoped Sara remembered to bring the revolver.

Rainey climbed at least a dozen cement steps to the double glass doors at the entrance of the Phoenix PD. Just inside she was scanned and her purse and briefcase x-rayed, before being allowed to proceed to a bullet-proofed area that stretched across the entire width of the room, save for a set of steel doors. The desk sergeant was just a tad overweight with thinning light brown hair. He looked up at Rainey and gave her a pleasant smile. He was sitting behind the screen, taking names and giving directions to visitors. His name tag read Sergeant Tim Williams. When Rainey stood in front of him and produced her driver's license, he looked briefly at it and checked it against a list of names before picking up the phone. Rainey assumed he called Sergeant Ames when the steel door opened and a diminutive uniformed female sergeant with olive colored skin and short curly black hair approached Rainey with a huge smile and an out-stretched hand.

Rainey felt over-dressed, but her anxiety level took a decided dip downwards at this second unexpected friendly greeting.

"Welcome to Arizona, Agent Walker. Welcome to Phoenix and welcome to Phoenix headquarters."

"Thank you," was all Rainey managed to get out before this very friendly sergeant said, "We are pleased you had time to drop by. I apologize for not telling you about our VIP parking. Did you have any problems finding a parking space?" Before Rainey could respond Sergeant Ames continued, "The desk sergeant will validate your parking, or if you prefer, I can have an officer move your vehicle to our reserved parking." Sergeant Ames held out her hand and seemed to be waiting for Rainey to produce her car keys.

"It's the blue Buick four-door parked across the street with Arizona plate 455682E," Rainey said, as the Sergeant spoke into the microphone attached to her shirt collar. Sergeant Ames left the keys with the desk sergeant who gave her a friendly wink and a hearty smile.

"All set?" Sergeant Ames said. Not really a question, so Rainey just nodded in the affirmative and followed her through the steel door.

"Everyone is so anxious to meet you Agent Walker. You're a real hero. So brave in taking out the Friday Stalker and you're not even a field agent! The guys in the bullpen keep saying that you're not like those stuck-up field agents we deal with every time a task force is set up."

Rainey didn't know how to answer…or even if an answer was expected. *Better just keep my mouth shut and listen. Sergeant Ames is a virtual deep information well.* Rainey just nodded and smiled from time to time as they walked down a long hallway. Offices were on each side and Rainey could see activity in almost every room.

"Major Billings has been waiting impatiently for you to arrive. No…you aren't late at all. It's just that we aren't making any headway in identifying a possible suspect. There aren't any leads and the perp is good…*real* good…at not leaving our crime scene technicians anything to collect. Our press officer has been stalling, but we can't keep saying "no comment." The public and press have already figured out we have a serial killer operating in Maricopa County and avoiding the fact is only making people angry and leading to rumors and stuff that just makes things more difficult."

"It can be difficult determining just how much information to make public…" Rainey began but Sergeant Ames continued as if Rainey hadn't said a word.

"The chief was in Major Billings' office last week, biting his head off. Kept yelling about wanting some results and something he could tell the press and public. That's when Major Billings called your boss and they decided that you could help because your boss says the Muslim community will talk to you. Our male officers can't get anywhere near the female Muslims and the males don't trust the police at all…a long history of distrust going back to before 9/11."

It had been over a decade since Rainey had lived in Arizona, and most likely the Muslim communities had changed just as Rainey had. She realized it wouldn't do much good to protest. Her boss had set her up, but good!

Sergeant Ames stopped at an elevator and Rainey followed her in. They stepped out on the third floor, walked down the hallway, and stopped abruptly in front of a door labeled Major H. W. Billings in gold and black stencil. Sergeant Ames' chatter stopped abruptly, too. She opened the door to a reception area. "This is my hangout," the sergeant said, walking past her desk, her name plate resting on one of its corners. The desk guarded another office door, and she knocked three times. The voice from within boomed "Enter." Sergeant Ames opened the door and both she and Rainey went through the doorway. Walking towards Rainey was the major. He stood nearly 6' 5" and was a very trim and muscular 220 pounds. His grey hair was Marine Corps cut, and it looked good on him. The major was dressed in a tailored, pin-striped Brooks Brothers suit with a gorgeous silk tie and he smelled delicious. That's the only way Rainey could describe him later to Sara.

"Good to meet you Agent Walker. Have a seat. I hope Sergeant Ames took care of your car and filled you in on a few of the issues I'm hoping you can help us with?"

Sergeant Ames blushed. Seems both her boss and Rainey had her correctly pegged as a walking information machine. Rainey smiled at her to ease her embarrassment and said, "Sergeant Ames has been very helpful and I appreciate the information, Major Billings."

"Let's not stand on ceremony. Everyone around here calls me HW when they think I'm not listening. The task force team has already dubbed you RW. Hope you won't take offense?"

Rainey relaxed and said, "RW is just fine. Can I ask what the HW stands for?"

Sergeant Ames covered her mouth and made a fair attempt at clearing her throat to stifle a giggle.

The major scowled at her, but it didn't last long. "My parents were both staunch Republicans and thought Hebert Walker

Bush Senior was the greatest president since Ronald Reagan." He laughed and his laugh was contagious, and in no time all three of them were laughing.

"You sure know how to break the ice," Rainey said, as she wiped her eyes.

"Well, now that I am at ease and you are at ease, we can get down to some serious business," HW said as he pushed a stack of bulging file folders across his desk towards Rainey. If you don't mind, I have assigned Sergeant Ames to be your liaison. You need anything, just tell her, and she will make sure I know and take care of things for you. Sometimes I get caught up in administrative matters, but Ames here knows how to track me down and she's persistent. She doesn't let anything get by me or leave my backside unprotected…she'll be as diligent in her efforts on your behalf, too."

"Thanks HW. I know Sergeant Ames and I will get along just fine. Thank you."

"That will be all for now, Sergeant Ames. I'll give you a call when RW here is ready to meet the team and visit the Scarf Killer murder room." Sergeant Ames smiled at Rainey and quietly closed the door as she left the major's office.

SKTF

"Nothing much else I have to cover right now, RW. I know you need some time to read the case files and meet the task force members. I wanted a private moment to give you some 'HW words of wisdom.' It won't be easy coming into the middle of a task force formed two months ago. Maybe even more difficult, as you don't usually work as a field agent, but we're here to give you all the support we can and to benefit from your expertise.

"I also wanted to tell you that taking out that killer was your only option. You did your job and saved the girl. Taking any life is never an easy thing. Don't second guess your decision or dwell on it. You showed a lot of courage that can't be planned or learned. It has been my pleasure meeting you. Do your best, will ya, 'cause this psycho needs to be stopped."

The major stood and walked towards Rainey. She stood up and they shook hands. "Thanks HW. Your words help and mean a lot." Rainey opened her briefcase and placed the copied case files inside.

Rainey passed through the doorway and saw Sergeant Ames waiting for her. The sergeant gave her a thumbs-up and motioned for Rainey to follow her.

Sergeant Ames stopped in front of an elevator, punched the Open button and explained that Major Crimes and Homicide

Divisions were located on the second floor. The Scarf Killer Task Force was assigned the largest conference room, which had been partitioned to provide a murder room and a briefing room. The conference rooms were located at the end of a very long hallway, with Major Crimes (MC) to the right and Homicide Division (HD) on Rainey's left. Records and Admin Staff were located within each division. Only Property and Evidence (P&E) was kept separate and located in the Department's Central Property and Evidence Bureau located in a separate building.

"The officers complain all the time about having to go back and forth to P&E but time and lots of mistakes proved that centrally locating the property and evidence reduced losses and improved accountability," Sergeant Ames said as she pushed a buzzer on the door with the paper sign labeled SKTF.

Rainey picked up on the fact that within the Phoenix PD police culture, use of acronyms to identify people's names, department locations, and even major cases was evidently popular. *Just like the feds*, she thought.

The animated discussions of the eight individuals seated around a very large conference table stopped abruptly as Rainey and Sergeant Ames walked through the door. Eight pairs of eyes inspected, weighed, and formed first impressions of Rainey. Sergeant Ames closed the door and said to the room of professionals, "Hi, you all. Meet RW."

"Hey there, Sarge, what took you so long?" A very tall and well-proportioned Phoenix lieutenant with gleaming gold bars pushed back his chair and made his way over to Rainey. He stuck out his hand and said, "Welcome to Phoenix PD and the task force. I'm Lieutenant Robert Jerald and I head up the task force under Major Billings." He made direct eye contact with Rainey. His look was measured, his voice firm with warmth.

Rainey hadn't known what to expect. She had heard all the stories about how local agency officers gave the cold shoulder to the FBI and resented the Bureau's butting in. She looked beyond

Lieutenant Jerald's shoulder and saw a room full of people smiling and nodding towards her.

Rainey shook the lieutenant's hand and walked with him as he guided her to the empty chair to his left at the conference table. *God, it feels good to sit down and not have everyone stare at me... even if the stares seem friendly,* thought Rainey as she eased her now heavy briefcase to the floor next to her chair.

The members of the task force introduced themselves clockwise around the table and stopped with Rainey. Again, eyes focused on her as the task force waited for her to introduce herself.

"I appreciate the warm welcome I have received from the Phoenix PD. Actually I didn't know what to expect coming in several months after this task force was organized." Rainey paused and then plunged into the gist of what she wanted these brave men and women to know about her and what she hoped to do to help them.

"Before the Bureau convinced me to sign up, I was a professor of anthropology and taught at NYU. It was a nice, safe, and rewarding career I very much enjoyed. I had a good friend in the Bureau working as a field agent out of the Profilers Division, and they needed a sketch artist like yesterday!" Rainey felt relief when she heard the chuckles of some of the task force members. "I had a minor degree in art, and my hobby is portrait sketching. I got a call from her boss asking me to help them out, and although I had some initial misgivings, I agreed to do what I could to help. Over a period of a couple of years, the Bureau began consulting me on cases involving portrait sketching and bone analysis and identification. I got interested in this field and took some FBI and scientific courses, and spent a lot of my extra time...make that every hour I wasn't teaching or sleeping...in the Bureau's Criminology Department learning about the various tools used on crime victims by their killers.

"When offered a full-time position with the Bureau, I accepted. I completed the training academy and received 'agent' status, but was assigned, by prior agreement, to work in the Bureau's Criminology Division doing what I do best…bone and tool analysis and an occasional sketching. I do civilian–type work though I am a sworn and trained law enforcement officer. I am usually not assigned to field work.

"How do I fit into this task force? What can I contribute? I grew up in Tempe. My grandmother was a Muslim and active in the Muslim community up until her death. She was, then and now, the only Muslim in my family. I am not Muslim, but grew up meeting many Muslims in the communities in Maricopa County. I worked all through high school at a local Phoenix Muslim food bank handing out food each week to the needy at their farmer's market. I had many Muslim playmates, spent time in their homes, and over the years, have maintained contact with a few Muslim friends still living in the local community. I still own the home my grandparents left me.

"Three months ago, I was involved in a serial killer case and I got shot. Hard for me to believe, but it happened. Three days ago, I was on leave and came home to Tempe to rest and let my shoulder heal. Two days ago, my boss called and asked…ah hmmm… *ordered* me to meet HW- Major Billings. My boss and your boss seem to think my connections with the Muslim community can help this task force with information gathering. I am here today meeting with you and will do what I can to help. My understanding from my boss and your boss is that I am here to serve as a consultant and not as an official field officer."

Rainey took a long drink from her water bottle. While waiting for a response from the task force, she opened her purse, took out her business cards and handed them to the Phoenix detective seated to her right. "Please feel free to call me at anytime on my cell number on the card here, or you can reach me at my home." Rainey gave her home address and noticed that Sergeant Ames wrote her name, RW, and her Tempe address and phone number on a white board attached to one of the briefing room walls.

"Thank you RW," Lieutenant Jerald said, taking over the meeting. "I wanted to add just a few things. First and most importantly, RW's connection to the SKTF needs to be kept within this room. Don't talk about it and refer to her only as RW in any notes and preliminary reports. No talking about RW with the girlfriend or boyfriend or spouse. You could jeopardize this investigation and you will face serious consequences if you mouth off to anyone, especially the media."

Rainey saw the task force members nodding their agreement.

"Secondly, RW has been much too modest about her work in the FBI. She single handedly took down the Friday Stalker and was shot in the line of duty saving the life of the last victim. She has worked with many other agencies on high profile cases offering her forensic expertise, as well as her police artist skills. She may not be labeled a field agent, but she is one of us, a sister in law enforcement, and she has paid her dues. Don't anyone forget that, and don't sell her value to this task force short." Lieutenant Jerald paused and smiled at Rainey.

"The formal meeting is now over. RW needs to visit the murder room and have some time to look over the case files. You can talk to her once she gets familiar with the setup." Lieutenant Jerald stood and again extended his hand to Rainey. She felt such relief having met the task force and having her role defined.

Just how she would be able to help remained to be seen. First she needed to read the case files and hear from the individual task force members. Hopefully they would point her in a direction that would get her the kind of information needed to advance the investigation.

The Facts

Rainey's stomach churned as she walked with Detective Carlos Ramirez around the screen partition. "Call me Carlos. We're all on first name basis unless you're a VIP—then we use initials. Very informal, as you can see by how most of us are dressed. The lieutenant just dressed up today to impress you," Carlos added with a wink.

"VIP…hmm…something I've never been accused of before," Rainey said with a smile. Carlos walked over to the first set of color photos and began pointing out the crime scenes and family-supplied photos. Rainey listened, only half concentrating. She was relieved when Harry, Officer Rather, approached and handed Rainey a manila folder.

"I put together some data we've been working with. A lot of it is derived from reviewing incident reports and then all of us brainstorming to identify similarities and differences in the victims." Harry handed her a second folder. "This folder has the results of our brainstorming efforts—what we know about the killer and what we don't know. We thought this would help get you up to speed a lot quicker than trying to individually pick our brains. That can come after you've had time to review the case files. If you want, Sergeant Ames can take you to P&E and you can look over the evidence from each crime scene. Identifying evidence for the killer and trace evidence from the crime scenes is pretty sparse, but the victims' clothing may be of interest to you."

"I'd like to look at the clothing, but I have an appointment in just a little over an hour at the Tempe mosque. My grandmother's old friend arranged for me to attend a weekly meeting for women, and I'm sure she called everyone who knew me and my grandmother so they could see me."

"That's perfect," Officer Cheryl White remarked. She had been standing close by and had not had an opportunity to speak to Rainey yet. "We haven't even been able to get the names of most of the Muslim women in the community fitting the age range and descriptions of the three victims. Maybe after the meeting, you can begin a list for contacting them individually?"

"Sounds like the beginning of a good plan," Rainey replied, giving Officer White a thumbs up and her goodbyes to other task force members as she headed for the exit.

Lieutenant Jerald caught up with Rainey before she walked out the door. "Glad I caught you. We'd like to return your rental and settle up your bill." He fished into his pants pocket and pulled out a set of car keys. "We're assigning you one of our undercover vehicles. If an officer in the field runs the plate for any reason, he'll know not to pull you over unless you indicate you need to speak to him. The payment for your rental will come from a Department crime fund. Enterprise can't trace it back to Phoenix PD. When you come to the Department for a SKTF meeting, go through the employee entrance in the back, and you can …maybe put that long hair up or in a ponytail and wear casual clothing, too." The lieutenant handed Rainey a Cardinals baseball cap. "You can use this and a pair of sunglasses." Rainey accepted the baseball cap and car keys with a grateful smile. "Sergeant Ames will show you where your wheels are in the back lot. Anything else you need for now?"

Rainey took mental inventory. "I think I've more than enough information to read tonight. I appreciate the loan of the vehicle, and I like my new hat. I'll give Sergeant Ames a call after my get together this afternoon. I don't know who will be there from my past and who will want to meet my grandma's granddaughter." Rainey tipped her new cap towards the lieutenant as the door to the task force room began to close behind her.

Rainey turned toward the elevator just as it opened and was greeted by Sergeant Ames. "All through for the day? Like the red baseball cap...it makes some kind of fashion statement with that linen suit and navy pumps," she said with a wink.

Rainey and the sergeant burst out laughing. Rainey juggled her purse, the now heavy briefcase, and the file folders from Officer White. "I think my day has just begun," Rainey said, looking at the information she had been given to absorb and process.

Before Sergeant Ames could respond, Rainey's non-departmental cell phone rang. Rainey quickly put down her briefcase and the file folders, opened her purse and took out the phone. Flipping it open she could see from the number that it was from Zarinah. Rainey put her index finger to her lips and Sergeant Ames nodded she understood.

"Salaams right back to you, Zarinah. I was just getting ready to head over to the masjid." Rainey was silent as she listened to Zarinah.

"No problem. I don't mind at all—I'm just surprised. Tomorrow after the afternoon prayer time is fine with me. I didn't think there would be that many of Grams' friends that would remember me." Rainey paused again to listen to Zarinah. "Really? The kids want me to sign their books? I'm...well I don't know what to say." Rainey laughed and said, "I think you're right. Anyone who knew Grams knows those books were about me and my friends." Rainey paused. "No...not at all. I think it will be fun meeting several generations of readers. Sounds like a lot of fun, actually.

Okay, until tomorrow afternoon. Yes... I can get to the masjid. Do you think it would be okay to bring my best girlfriend with me? She's flying in tomorrow morning to spend a few days. I know she'd love to come. Yes, and thanks for bringing a scarf for her, too. Salaams."

"You heard?' Rainey asked Sergeant Ames.

"Pretty much. Your girlfriend would be Agent Sara James?"

"That's right, and she really is my best friend," Rainey replied, as she stooped to pick up the files and briefcase.

"Let's go get you your new wheels," Sergeant Ames said, pressing the down arrow.

Sergeant Ames waved at Rainey as she drove out of the employee car lot. When she lost sight of Rainey's car, she quickly pulled out her cell phone and speed dialed Major Billings.

"Ames, this better be important. I'm on my way to Staff."

"Did you know Agent Walker's grandmother wrote and published a book series, and the main character in the books is Agent Walker?" Sergeant Ames said with smugness the major heard, but chose to ignore.

"You have five minutes. I'm on the third floor."

"I'll take it," Sergeant Ames said as she ran towards the stairwell. She wasn't about to waste precious seconds waiting on the elevator. When the major said five minutes, he usually meant three.

Major Billings was waiting at the top of the third floor stairwell when Sergeant Ames cleared the landing leading to the last five steps. "You must know something important connected to what you just told me," the Major said.

"Seems Agent Walker is a minor celebrity within the Muslim community because of her grandmother's book series. The meeting this afternoon was delayed so her grandmother's friend...ah... Zarinah Awad...can arrange for more people to meet and greet

Agent Walker. Some will be bringing their kids so Agent Walker can sign copies of the kids' books. This friend Zarinah is turning a small meeting with a few friends into a major community event overnight."

"Call Lieutenant Jerald. He'll need to get camera surveillance setup. Many of the Muslim women don't drive so we can get photos and film with husbands and wives together and run the license plates, too. We'll have some home addresses or work addresses to work with. Get a copy of those books and read them. I want a synopsis on each one. Have the first one ready tomorrow...and Ames, no need to tell Agent Walker about the surveillance tomorrow. Information to Agent Walker is to be on a need-to-know basis."

"You want me to tell Lieutenant Jerald to hold off on those subpoenas for the membership records of each mosque? The mosque leaders, I think they are called imams, have been uncooperative and serving the subpoenas isn't going to improve matters," Sergeant Ames said while glancing at her wrist watch.

"Yes, good idea. I was just about to mention that. Tell him let's wait and see what kind and how much information Agent Walker can turn up. This community event is the first positive break we've had all week." The major paused as he turned from her and said over his shoulder,

"Sergeant Ames?"

"Major?"

"Enjoy your quiet evening at home reading." The major strode down the hallway. Sergeant Ames was almost sure she heard him chuckle.

Rainey missed the late afternoon traffic, for which she was grateful. It would have taken an extra hour on the freeway from Phoenix traveling east to Tempe and home. After exiting the 202 and traveling south on Priest, Rainey began looking for a fast-food place to grab some supper. She was too tired to cook and still had a long evening of reading ahead of her. Spotting a Wendy's to her right, Rainey slowed and made a right turn into the drive-thru. A burger, fries, and chocolate shake was just what she wanted, though not necessarily what she needed, she admitted to herself.

Rainey turned into the carport driveway and turned off the ignition. Her department cell phone rang. It was Sara.

"Rainey, how ya doing? Meeting go okay? Did you get the cold shoulder?" Sara, as usual, piled on her questions without pausing for a response. Rainey waited. "I got an early morning, non-stop flight on American and should arrive at 7 AM. I should get a good five hours sleep, as I paid for a first-class upgrade." Sara paused.

"I'm fine, Sara. The meetings went really well. I am officially a consultant to the Phoenix task force and everyone was as nice and as helpful as can be. I'll meet your plane, we can have some breakfast, and I'll tell you all about it. Be prepared to go to a local mosque with me tomorrow afternoon. My grandmother's friend has arranged a meet and greet with the Muslim community...and I'll explain that tomorrow, too. Be sure to pack a long skirt and long sleeved blouse and make it a conservative neckline, please. The meeting is at the local mosque and I want everyone there feeling comfortable when looking at us. Okay?"

"Sure, no problem."

"I'm gonna cut this short, Sara. I've got a humongous cheeseburger, large fries, and a Frosty waiting on me, and a pound or two of reports to read before tomorrow."

"See you tomorrow," Sara replied and rang off.

The Killer

Pacing did nothing to relieve the killer's neck muscle tension, or to stop the buzzing sound growing louder by the minute. "Come on, you idiot pig. Answer my email." The killer had been cultivating the pig for months now through a local Girls and Boys Club where he volunteered each week. They emailed each other almost daily. The cop's erratic work schedule made it impossible for them to meet often. Good for the cop, because the killer's hands itched to feel a knife through his soft, doughy belly, twist it, and hear the pig squeal. Soon...soon his life would drain away, and he would die in agony. But for now, the pig was useful.

"You've got mail." The announcement interrupted the killer's pacing. Clicking the email icon with a satisfied smile, the killer thought, *That's my boy...only a few minutes past shift change. I'll play nice and be the understanding friend.*

Cop message:
> *No can do. Got graveyard shift. What about meeting for breakfast? Some exciting developments...some bigwig from back east met with them. Don't know much more right now. No one is talking. I know you need a break on this story, but I'm working on it. Wish I had more to offer.*

Response:

Graveyard shift…that's the pits. Breakfast about 9 AM at the usual place okay? Don't worry about it. We'll figure out something. Be safe. See ya in the morning."

"Whiner…fool… imbecile!" A slender finger clicked the Send key as anger radiated from the killer like white heat. A grimace spread and contorted the killer's classic good looks into a grotesque mask of ugliness. The laptop lid slammed closed.

When they'd met three months ago at the club, the pig had talked a lot about his connections downtown at Phoenix PD headquarters. The stupid kids just ate it up. That was a small miscalculation; the pig's confinement to shift work should have indicated that he was nothing but a grunt. Tonight's bit of news about a bigwig, though…if the pig could provide more useful information, he just might live awhile longer.

The pig had been completely taken in by the killer's role as a free-lance reporter looking for the big break, who was also dedicated to helping underprivileged kids. It didn't take much to get the pig talking about his being unnoticed by the brass for eighteen years. He'd whined about needing to be part of an important case that would get him promoted to detective and out of uniform and shift work.

No, it didn't take much—a few dinners and lots of emails boosting the slug's ego—to convince him that working together, they could break a big story on the Scarf Killer, featuring the pig as a hero.

"I need to calm down. Relax. Have to get some sleep. Can't show up for breakfast looking all haggard." A sly look crossed the killer's face. Reaching inside the pillow's slipcover, the killer carefully pulled out five swatches of long hair. Each swatch was carefully tied at both ends to keep each intact and separate. The killer raised each bundle of hair closer and breathed in through flaring nostrils. The scent of the victims made the killer's pulse race with excitement.

The pillow was the killer's special trophy case; every time it was touched, indescribable excitement surged inside the killer and left calm in its wake. Having the trophies just out of sight heightened the thrill and upped the ante should the place ever be searched. And with each new trophy there was a touchable, sensual reminder that another deceiver was exterminated...wiped off the face of the Earth!

Missing Pieces

Rainey rubbed her eyes and stretched. She had been reading and making notes for four hours. A cup of tea might take away the bad taste in her mouth. Returning to the dining room table with her tea, Rainey pushed the last file to her left and moved the yellow legal pad to the center of her workspace. She had not yet read the task force's victims comparisons and the killer profile, wanting first to create her own to compare to, and add to, the task force's conclusions. Rainey had also listed some questions for information she hadn't found in any of the case files. Rainey looked at page one of her victim comparison:

- *All Female*
- *All younger than 35 years of age*
- *All married*
- *All had young children…public or private school? home school?*
- *All English speaking…speak another language?*
- *All wore hijab…Did they wear a veil? What about gloves?*
- *All lived in Maricopa County*
- *Attended different mosques: Phoenix, Tempe, and Chandler*
- *None were sexually molested…nothing resulted from the autopsies.*

- *Where are husbands employed? Skills?*
- *When did they last travel outside the USA?*
- *Did their wives (family) travel with them?*
- *Victims: Raised Muslim or converted to Islam?*
- *High school or college graduates?*
- *2 killed in their homes; 1 killed in a Wal-Mart…the 1ˢᵗ known victim*
- *2 poisoned; 1 stabbed to death-first known victim*
- *All had their long hair cut off with scissors—make of scissors undetermined*
- *All had their faces mutilated. 2 with a serrated knife... common steak knife found in almost any home. Victim 1's was not mutilated with knife used to stab her to death. Killer didn't have time?*
- *Face wounds of Victims 2 & 3 are post mortem.*
- *All are stay-at-home moms*
- *Killer called police and reported victim 2 and 3. The first victim found in the Wal-Mart restroom.*
- *Victim 1's toddler in stroller present and found screaming by female shopper finding the body in a closed stall.*

Did the killer not have a chance to call in the first killing before it was discovered? Would this be a reason for changing the kill zone to the victim's home?

Did the victims know each other? No…not according to the husbands…but would the husbands know who their wives' Muslim sister-friends were?

Note→ Maybe…but probably not. Other sisters would know.

Victim 1: Nancy Elaine Holder AKA Umm Amatullah Ali, 5'4", 155 lbs. Bro/Bld. Cau. born in the USA. DOB: 10/04/1980. No Social Security number listed

Notes on Vic 1:
> *Convert to Islam. How many years?*
> *Using husband's last name: Husband's name: Ahmet Ali,*
> *   what country?*
> *Unusual…Muslim women retain their father's last name*
> *   when they marry. Maybe she took her husband's name*
> *   to fit in better in the community?*
> *Did anyone interview her non-Muslim family members?*
> *Did she frequently shop at Wal-Mart?*

Victim 2: Aneerah Mohamed AKA Umm Yusuf, 5'6', 140 lbs.
Bro/Blk, Cau., born in USA-2nd generation: ancestry?
country? DOB: 03/15/1978, No Social Security number
listed

Notes on Vic 2:
> *Raised Muslim; last name different from husband's last*
> *   name: His name: Adnan Nassar*
> *What other language/s spoken?*

Victim 3: Saaleha Abdullah AKA Umm Ibrahim, 5'5", 160
lbs. Bro/Blk, Cau., born in USA 2nd generation: ancestry/
country? DOB: 09/16/1981
No Social Security number listed
Husband: Fahd Al-Marwani: nationality/country?

Notes→
> *All husbands non-natural born USA citizens. What country/*
> *   nationality? Is this important?*
> *Victims and Muslim family members - Sunni Muslim. No*
> *   conflict between sects such as Shia and Sunni.*

Question: Does this look like a Muslim killing Muslims? My gut
tells me No. Nothing in the case files points to this.

*Local and county law enforcement databases came up negative…
victims are not in their database systems. AFIS and NCIC reports
negative for all three victims. Not in any system…not even for a
parking ticket, but all three had a driver's license*

Rainey flipped the page to read the Killer Unsub Profile she
came up with:

- *One or two unsubs?…I think only one acting alone*
- *Male or female? Unknown?*
- *Muslim or non-Muslim? Hate crimes by a non-Muslim
  directed at Muslims?*
- *Possible unsub height from angle of stab wound-1st victim:
  5'7" to 6'…could be wearing shoes with built up heels*
- *No fingerprints found…wears some kind of gloves; no trace
  evidence.*
- *No fibers collected…careful about type of clothing worn*
- *Victim's homes not broken into…Did the victims know the
  killer?*
- *What reason would cause a Muslim woman to open her
  front/back door when her husband was not home?*
- *For Victims 2 & 3: Access to poison…nothing special
  required…garden pesticides*
- *Victims 2 & 3 ingested poisoned baked goods…brought by
  the killer day of death*
- *Killer called it in…killer present…wants to see victims die.*
- *Uses disposable cell phones…smart*
- *Shreds their head scarves and covers their mutilated faces
  with the scarves. Is covering their faces significant? Like
  the victim is hiding her face to hide her ugliness from the
  world? Does the disfigurement mean something else to the
  killer?*
- *Cutting hair and taking it - Trophy to relive the killings…
  but why hair?*

- *All three killed before 5 PM…Killer disguised? Bold to operate in the daytime*
- *Any threats to the victims prior to being killed? No*
- *What connects the 3 victims to the killer?*
- *Are the husbands being targeted through them or is it just the victims as the targets?*
- *Killer's motive?*

Rainey reread the last piece of information, perhaps the key to finding the killer. *This piece of information would be withheld from the public when, if ever, it became known*, Rainey thought. *Smart, like most serial killers, and arrogant—SK thinks the police have a collective inferior intellect.*

Rainey considered SK's calling card—a yellow Post-it note stuck at the base of each victim's neck. *Taunting the police*, she thought. The killer had proclaimed after each killing that it would not be the last. The three notes read:

3 of 10
4 of 10
5 of 10

Rainey finished her notes:

- *What was significant about 10? Why not 8 or 12 or 20?*
- *What about 1 of 10 and 2 of 10? 10 Victims? No other victims have been found in Arizona.*
- *Elsewhere in the USA-similar killings? None reported using the SK killer and victim profiles.*
- *Has the killer moved on or is the killer still in Arizona?*
- *The numbers and letters were cut from a magazine or some ordinary paper document and pasted to each post-it note. Note→ Check with crime lab ref paper used.*

- *Post-it notes are sold almost anywhere and were bought in the hundreds of thousands. This killer wasn't leaving the cops much to work with.*

Rainey felt a chill travel down her spine. They could expect five more brutal slayings. "My God!" Rainey exclaimed as she finished rereading the case files and reviewing her notes.

There must be some common link, other than the fact that the three victims were female Muslims, but what was it?

Rainey looked at the pile of reports and found the three files containing the medical examiner reports. She flipped open the file on Victim 1 and as she read began taking her own notes.

Victim 1 or 3 of 10
- *Victim fought her attacker*
- *Defensive knife wounds on both hands and arms*
- *Cause of death a single knife wound inserted directly into the heart by a long sharp instrument. Possibly a knife used by a doctor or surgeon. All wounds were made prior to death*
- *Hair cut off with common scissors…most likely after death*
- *Victim found with head scarf placed over the face, but the face was <u>not mutilated. Why?</u>*
- *No sexual assault*
- *No drugs-alcohol in victim's system*
- *No hair or fiber transfer that can be attributed to the killer*
- *Post-it note placed under chin on the neck of the victim*

Notes:
- *Did the victim know the unsub?*
- *Does the unsub have medical training or access to medical instruments?*
- *Does this mean the mutilations of Vic 2 & 3 are something*

new to the killer's pattern or was Victim 1 not mutilated
because there wasn't time? Was the unsub maybe worried
about someone coming into the restroom?

- Was this an impulse killing or planned to take place in that
  location?
- A child of the victim was present, but left physically
  unharmed. Significance?
- Unsub did not call police and report the killing of Victim 1
  like Victim 2 & 3. Could this mean Victim 1 was found too
  quickly for the killer to have time to call it in?
- Was the killer present in the store watching?
- Could the killer's name be on the list of shoppers the police
  interviewed or did the unsub get away before the police
  arrived?...too smart to hang around...?
- How did the killer leave the store without the blood of the
  victim on killer's clothes not being noticed by any shoppers?
- Did the unsub bring a change of clothes and cleaning
  supplies in a Murder Kit?
- No blood found in any sinks or drains or anywhere in the
  restroom except the victim's blood
- Dozens of fingerprints were found-public restroom. No way
  to link them to anyone. All usable fingerprints lifted by
  the technicians, run through NCIC and AFIS, but no hits.
  Killer was wearing gloves or doesn't have an arrest record.

Victim 2 or 4 of 10
- No evidence that the victim fought the killer; no bruising,
  injuries prior to death
- Cause of death from cyanide poisoning within minutes of
  poison ingestion
- Poison contained in samples of chocolate brownies found
  on the kitchen table and partially consumed chocolate
  brownies the victim ingested. Frothing at the mouth and

partially consumed brownie found on the victim's face and floor where victim found.

- *Staging: Killer positioned the victim on her back after death occurred.*
- *Victim's face mutilated post mortem. 6 slashes of varying length made with a serrated steak knife found on the floor next to the victim. Knife is one of a set of 8 owned by Victim…verified by husband.*
- *Victim's head scarf covering the victims face had traces of cyanide brownies and blood from post mortem wounds.*
- *No drugs or alcohol found in the victim other than the poison*
- *No sexual assault*
- *No hair or fiber transfer that can be attributed to the killer*

Notes:

- *No forced entry into victims home; was let in; left by front or back door*
- *Assumption: the victim knew the killer*
- *Children present in the home at time of killing, left unharmed, but too young to question about any "visitor" of mother*
- *Body position, head scarf covering face, hair cut off with scissors (brought by killer) same as Victim 1.*
- *Post-it note placed by killer under chin on the neck of the victim*
- *Assumption: Killer brought the chocolate brownies to the victim's home, left uneaten brownies. No concern if anyone else in the household ate any of the brownies?*

Victim 3 or 5 of 10

- *Nothing is significantly different from Victim 2 in ME report or crime scene.*

- *Almost identical methods used by killer.*
- *Again there was no forced entry*
- *Again children present in home/location of killing.*
- *Again there was post mortem mutilation; kitchen knife used was owned by the victim.*
- *Again cause of death was cyanide poisoned chocolate brownies.*

Questions:
- *Wasn't Victim 3 aware of how Victim 2 died? If yes, then why would she allow the killer into her home and accept the brownies and begin eating one? If no, there is a real problem in the community with not getting information to members to protect the women.*
- *Victims 2 & 3 almost certainly knew their killer. Did Victim 1 know the killer?*
- *No pattern for length of time between killings but all victims killed before 5 PM - is this significant?*
- *Why did the killer change the method of killing from knife to poison?*
- *What about 1 of 10 and 2 of 10...are they deceased victims killed in another location/s? Or is the killer just toying with the police-trying to cause confusion?*
- *Motive?*

Rainey rubbed the back of her neck, raised her eyes from her notes and looked longingly at the double French doors leading to the patio. Despite her desire to continue, she was just too tired to read the task force profiles tonight. It was time to call it a day. Rainey wanted to go out and sit in the porch swing, but instead carried the cold cup of tea to the kitchen, poured it down the drain, and placed it in the dishwasher. She turned out the kitchen and dining room lights, secured the doors, and headed down the hallway to a well earned sleep.

The Stranger

Rainey scanned the individuals coming towards the terminal opening from the American Airline flight that had landed. Sara, at just 5'4" would be easily lost in a group of hurrying passengers, but for that near white cap of tousled hair that she usually kept covered with a Bureau baseball cap. On assignments, Sara often had to use a wig. Rainey still remembered the dustup when the Bureau had tried to get Sara to dye her hair. Sara had insisted she could disguise herself well enough without a dye job. She told her boss he'd never recognize her. To prove her point, Sara put on one of the natural hair wigs, used some creative makeup techniques, added a decrepit hat, and wearing some street clothes bought from Goodwill and drug through a garbage dump, Sara sat on a bus bench outside the Bureau building one morning with a bag of trash. Nobody going in or out of the building gave her a second glance, not even her boss. When her boss and one of the agents left the building on their way to lunch, Sara made a small scene and begged some change from them as they walked by the bench. Her boss, typically, looked around for a security guard to remove her from the proximity, but he didn't hang around once the security guard arrived.

Sara identified herself to the security guard and explained the joke. She asked him to take a photo of her and he was willing to do anything the saucy female agent wanted, once he took a good look at her violet eyes and mischievous grin. Sara then did a quick change of clothes and makeup, returned to the bench near the Bureau building, and waited for her boss to return from lunch. Upon approaching the building, he asked if she'd been waiting long. Sara responded that she had been there all morning and asked why he had tried to get her removed by security. Sara handed him the Polaroid without even trying to hide her smirk. He didn't mention Sara coloring her hair again.

The stream of passengers dwindled and then there was no one entering the terminal from the plane. Momentarily Rainey wondered if she had come to the wrong gate or got the flight number or time wrong. A grin spread across her face as she rescanned the faces of the fliers. A woman conservatively dressed in a brown tailored suit with a fake alligator bag and matching fake alligator high heels was headed her way. The woman looked to be in her late thirties, with a medium brown page-boy streaked with premature white hair at both temples. The woman wore wire-rimmed glasses and hunched her shoulders slightly as she walked.

"Can you help me, miss?" the woman said before she grabbed Rainey and hugged her.

Rainey was laughing so hard her eyes teared up. "And you are?"

"I'm a librarian by profession and on a short vacation visiting an old college chum in her hometown. I always wanted to visit Arizona. Think we can get away from things long enough to see the Grand Canyon?" It was Sara alright; she always ended what she was talking about with a question.

"You almost had me fooled. I think it's the high heels. I was looking for a shrimp-boat," Rainey said once she got her laughter under control.

"Let's get out of here. I want to hear all about your meetings yesterday, the case, and your celebrity event at the mosque. I'm starved. Where are we gonna have breakfast? Can we go someplace where I can get some authentic southwest cuisine?"

Rainey linked her arm with Sara. "First we get your luggage and then we get breakfast."

The waitress approached with the coffee pot. Rainey and Sara both put a hand over the top of their cups indicating they had had enough. "I was going to ask you how you are doing, but you are simply glowing, Rainey. Three days here and that washed-out dazed look is gone. All this Arizona sunshine seems to agree with you, or is it something else?"

Rainey paused in what she was going to say and thought about Sara's words. She looked better? Rainey realized that even though she had been busy from the moment her plane landed three, or was it four days ago....she didn't feel tired. She felt energized and alive. She didn't feel guilty to be alive either, and had no nightmare last night. She had slept soundly.

Without voicing these thoughts to Sara, she told her, "Don't turn around quickly. Act naturally. Drop your spoon or something and when you pick it up glance over to your left. There is a *very* good looking man seated at a table drinking a cup of coffee. He's been glancing our way since he came into the restaurant. He even smiled at me once. I think he's watching us."

"He's probably watching *you* and trying to flirt," was Sara's response, but her curiosity got the better of her and she did what Rainey asked her to do. "Wow! He's a hunk," Sara exclaimed.

"Be quiet," Rainey said, and she wasn't smiling. Her face was serious and her brow was creased.

"I saw him at the airport terminal and then again in the car park. I think he followed us. I also think I saw him yesterday when I stopped at a convenience store. His good looks are too distinctive to be easily forgotten."

"That's for sure. Are you thinking this hottie has been following you for two days? Why? That's what we need to be thinking about... he fits right in with the jeans, western shirt and belt buckle. His sun-streaked hair and tanned skin indicate he spends a lot of time outdoors. But I know what you're thinking—it's just too much of a coincidence that he'd be in the same three places as you," Sara said.

"It's almost as if he wants me to know he's following me. He's been so obvious about it," Rainey said as she slowly stood up.

"What are you doing?" Sara asked in a low whisper knowing full well what Rainey was up to.

"I'm gonna walk over there, introduce myself, and ask him why he has been following me for two days. Watch my back. If he tries anything funny in this very public place I'd be really surprised."

Sara knew better than to argue with Rainey. She turned her chair deliberately to face the man, as Rainey approached his table at an angle so as not to block Sara's view. Sara watched as the man seemed to instinctively place his hands on top of the table in plain view. Sara watched his hands. It was too far a distance for Sara to hear what was being said, so she watched as Rainey nodded her head twice, and the man picked up what looked like a business card and handed it to Rainey. Rainey nodded again, turned around and walked back towards Sara.

Sara kept her eyes trained on the man. He stood up, placed some bills from his wallet on the table, and then he exited the restaurant without a backwards glance.

"What was that all about?" Sara asked, as her adrenalin began to subside and pulse slowed to normal.

"That was Captain Jonathan Daniels, US Army, and he was not hitting on me…that is for sure," Rainey said. The crease and worried look on Rainey's face hadn't changed.

"What did he say?" Sara asked, and this time she kept it to one question.

"Sara, he addressed me as Agent Walker and introduced himself by giving his name only. Then he said he was glad I picked up on the fact that he had made himself so obvious."

"He admitted to following you?"

"Yes. He even brought up the task force, but was quick to say he was not a member and was not known to any member of the task force."

"What'd you say?" Sara didn't know whether to feel excitement or dread at this point.

"I asked him what he wanted from me. Said he had a reason for following me and setting up this meeting here. I didn't make any comment about the task force."

"Did he tell you what he wanted?"

"No, he skirted the question and said, 'I'll be in touch. I have information, but am not at liberty to disclose it now. You have information I need that I don't want to obtain directly from the task force.' I told him that without knowing anything at all about him, I would not be meeting him at anytime in the future, discussing the time of day, or anything else with him. I told him to back off, and if I saw him again I would be reporting him to my boss."

"What did he say to that?"

"The idiot just smiled and handed me his business card. He said it was a real pleasure meeting me and he'd be in touch. Can you believe it?" Rainey paused. "I'm worried though. How did he know about my connection with the task force? He didn't seem at all worried when I said I'd have my boss check him out. He knows I mean the FBI."

"So why all the mystery? Why doesn't he want the task force to know about him? What can his involvement be? Is it personal, or is the military somehow involved in this serial killer case?" Sara ran out of questions, giving Rainey the opportunity to speak.

"I don't like this one bit. *I* didn't even know about the case before I arrived here." She looked accusingly at Sara, who had the grace to blush.

"What's printed on his business card?" Sara asked. Rainey tossed it across the table to Sara.

Rainey saw Sara's perplexed look. "That's it? His rank, name, military designation, and a phone number with the hand printed words, 'Call me when you need me'?"

"What do you plan to do about this? Tell the task force commander? Call the boss?" Sara asked.

"I think he already slipped up. I don't think he recognized you as an FBI agent. I don't think he believes I will tell you anything. He accepts the disguise you created as fact. So… let me ask you something. What are you going to do about this? I know the boss sent you out here to babysit me." Rainey looked directly into Sara's eyes and waited for her to try and deny it.

Sara's drumming her fingers on the table signaled that she was struggling to come to a decision. "Department regulations require me to report this to the boss and run a check on your captain through normal channels. But…my gut tells me we should hold off."

Rainey let out a sigh of relief. "I agree, Sara. We don't know enough about the good captain and I'd like to nose around a little first before we blow the whistle. I don't trust him one inch. He knows something about this case that us non-military don't, and I mean to find out what it is."

The Celebrity

Rainey received a call from Sergeant Ames to arrange going to P&E the next day to examine the evidence from the three crime scenes. Sara planned to use her time reading case files, reviewing Rainey's notes, and making some notes of her own. While Rainey met with the task force tomorrow, Sara planned to use her own sources to begin checking on the mysterious captain.

"All ready, Sara? My, don't you look prim and proper," Rainey teased as Sara walked into the living room and twirled in a circle for Rainey's inspection.

"Once we get there, I'm going to look foolish trying to put on a head scarf properly," Sara complained.

"Oh, Sara. No one would think you looked foolish. Anyways you don't need to be concerned. I talked with Zarinah while you were in the shower. The event is being held on the outdoor terrace just west and next door to the mosque. We won't be going inside so we won't need to put on a head scarf. Wearing a head scarf wasn't required in the first place. I just thought we'd wear one out of respect for their place of worship. Funny thing though. The first day I arrived and went to the restaurant across the street from the mosque to wait until Zarinah brought me the house keys…well I looked at the mosque, but I didn't even notice that the old Islamic school building was torn down and the space is now converted into a large, partially covered terrace. Zarinah told me many events like their semi-annual bazaars are held outdoors in the terrace area."

"Well that's a big relief for me. Just what are we, I mean you, going to be doing at this event?"

"Zarinah said that this small get-together with some of my and my grandmother's old friends has turned into a community event. She said there will be food to eat…remember not to sit with any of the men and mostly those coming will just give their salaams and exchange some small talk with me."

"And what does it mean—'give their salaams'?"

"It's an expression that means greeting somebody with 'peace,'" Rainey said and continued, "I understand that many of the children will be bringing their copies of the books my grandmother wrote and published…and incidentally are still selling… for me to sign. I really think this is more about remembering my grandmother than it is about me. My being here is a good excuse for the community to get together and socialize," Rainey said, and grinned at Sara.

"Now that's something I never expected. My knowledge of Muslims is so limited, and what I do know has little to do with how regular Muslims live."

"Keep in mind, Sara, that many in the Muslim community are scared. Three Muslim women have been brutally slain—two in their homes with their children present at the time. Add to this the anger at the delay in burial and need for the autopsies, and the Muslim community is not real happy. Three women are dead and the police don't have a thing to tell the families or the community. The killer is still at large."

"Why did the Muslims object to the autopsies?" Sara asked.

"Not all of them did, but no one but the husband should see a wife unclothed, and when a death occurs, Muslim women who have been taught how to wash and prepare a female body for burial do this. If no women are available, then it becomes the husband's or a blood relative's duty to the deceased. A Muslim is supposed to be buried within twenty four hours following death absent exigent circumstances, so each autopsy caused a delay, which caused anxiety on top of the heartache and fear."

"This doesn't explain why the community leaders and family aren't cooperating with the investigators. Their refusal to provide information is just hampering the investigations," Sara said.

"The Phoenix cops responding to the first murder at the Wal-Mart were overheard making crude remarks while waiting on the detectives and CIS technicians. One of them remarked that it was no big loss as there was one less terrorist. This got back to the family and Muslim leadership. When the detectives showed up for interviews they got doors slammed in their faces."

"I bet the media had a heyday reporting those comments," Sara stated. "I remember reading a couple 'letters to the editor' and most were not too sympathetic until the third killing, and then even the diehard racists seemed to tone down their jabs at the Muslims."

"That's what Zarinah told me. She said it didn't help much when the Chief of Police made a personal visit to each family. He called each of the eight imams in the Phoenix-Metro region, too, but this did nothing but cause more hard feelings. The Muslims viewed his actions as being politically motivated."

"This is a real can of worms back in Washington," Sara remarked. "The brass is expecting you to get some fast results and convince the community to provide information for the investigations."

"I am not Muslim or an insider, Sara. I have a toe in the doorway. Zarinah loved my grandmother and she loves me. She arranged this community event because she didn't want me to be at a disadvantage in case any Muslim displayed bad manners and said anything to me today. She's a smart lady and she wants answers about these killings more than anyone, and knows refusing to cooperate with the police isn't helping," Rainey said.

"All this just complicates the serial killer investigations." Sara said.

Rainey nodded agreement. "Just remember, Sara, that the Muslims you see and meet today are not greeting Agent Rainey Walker. They are coming out to see the granddaughter of a beloved Muslimah—someone many respected in life and pray for since her death."

"Understood," Sara said nodding her head.

"Taking into consideration the killings and issues I just told you about, you are gonna get exposed today to "regular" Muslims...see how most of the billion-plus Muslims in the world today behave. You'll see some differences, but I think you'll see a lot more similarities to non-Muslims than you would have thought possible."

Sara thought about the task force and wanted to tell Rainey. "Rainey?"

Rainey looked at Sara expectantly and waited for her to continue.

Sara wanted to tell Rainey about the surveillance operation of the task force. The SKTF commander had called DC Britt and given him an update, and DC had called Sara. Sara felt like a worm.

Sara had told DC last night when she reported in that Rainey looked and was acting like her old self. There seemed to be no reason to walk on eggs around her anymore or to keep anything about the investigation from her. But DC either didn't believe her, or there was an ulterior reason for keeping Rainey in the dark. Either Rainey was a member of the task force or she wasn't. Sara did not like how things were panning out and most definitely was still worried about that fine-looking unknown, the captain.

"Ah... nothing, Rainey," Sara replied and gave her an overly bright smile.

Rainey pretended to accept her friend's behavior as nothing unusual. She didn't press Sara, but Rainey was concerned. Sara was keeping something from her...holding back. Did her best friend trust her? Was she under orders to babysit Rainey, or was there something else going on?

Rainey gathered up the empty cups and saucers and carried them to the kitchen to cover any negative body language Sara might pick up on. *What is going on? First I get a royal welcome from the PPD. A PPD major's personal aid is assigned to be at my beck and call. Sara shows up for a mini vacation and to 'just help out,' and yesterday the mysterious captain introduces himself and leaves me a cryptic message to call him when I need help?* Rainey's stomach began to knot. *Maybe I'm not trusted by the task force, my boss, or even my best friend. Was it the trauma and my reaction to it? No... it couldn't be...but...*Rainey had to face the possibility that her grandmother being a Muslim and Rainey having been part of the Muslim community while growing up had something to do with the distrust. *Boy, that stinks.*

Rainey walked back into the living room and smiled at her best friend. "Let's get this show on the road. And Sara...just be yourself and relax. If you want to be of some help today, try and remember the names of the women you meet. Oh... and don't put out your hand to the men to shake. Just nod your head and smile."

"I did attend the sensitivity training and a basic Islam etiquette class," Sara sputtered uncomfortably. *Serves her right,* Rainey thought, hiding her grin as they headed out the door.

As Rainey turned onto the street and approached the mosque, she saw two teen-aged boys standing in a parking space. One, then both, began waving her into the parking spot where they were standing. "Now that's service," Sara said and grinned at Rainey.

"I didn't think earlier. You'll probably have some trouble picking up on everyone's names. Don't worry about it. I'm really hoping I'll see some women I used to know and hopefully get invited to their homes for a visit."

"I'll just listen and smile and maybe pickup on some conversations. If I hear anything I'll let you know and perhaps you can make the contact. Would that work?" Sara asked.

"Sounds good. Mainly I am hoping Muslims from other mosque communities show up so when I approach anyone, especially from the Phoenix and Chandler Muslim communities, I won't get the cold shoulder. Muslims love gossip even though they try real hard not to backbite."

"Muslims don't backbite?" Sara questioned.

"Yup. They try not to. It's considered a sin, as well as darned impolite," explained Rainey with a smile.

"But sharing information about you and this event would be okay?"

Rainey grinned and nodded as she put the car gear in park and switched off the ignition. "Here goes. I see Zarinah and her welcoming party. Jeez...there must be a couple hundred people here, not counting all the kids!"

Sara and Rainey got out of the car and were met by salaams and smiles. Shy children hid behind their mothers' skirts, but the older ones looked with open curiosity at the two guests. Sara noticed that most of the men gave a friendly nod of greeting but their gazes did not linger. She was surprised by the kaleidoscope of colors and styles of dress by the Muslim women. Most of the men were dressed casually...like non-Muslim men in slacks and dress or pullover shirts.

The purr of Zarinah's wheelchair stopped as she reached up to give Rainey a hug. "As salaam'alaykum, Rainey. Welcome Sara," Zarinah said, charming both with her beautiful smile.

Zarinah pointed to a group of young female teens and women standing near a semi-circle of chairs setup a short distance from the tables and chairs ready for everyone to use when "time to eat" was announced. "See the sister in the red and grey abeya and matching hijab? She's Sister Debora's daughter, Laila. She's here visiting Camelia's relatives. Camelia and her mother, Sis Judy, are still living in Egypt, but the family still has the restaurant here."

"Camelia." Rainey's face softened as she said the name softly with regret.

"Don't you go feeling bad because maybe you haven't been able to stay in touch with your childhood friends, Rainey. Come with me. Laila has been impossible while waiting to meet Hijabie Rose."

"Hijabie Rose?" Sara asked softly.

"It's the name of the main book character in my grandmother's book series. Camelia and I are characters in those books."

"Wow! You never said a word. Not one word!" Sara was impressed and just a tad put off that Rainey had failed to tell her about that huge chunk of her life.

Rainey said irritably, "I told you my grandmother was Muslim and I told you she was an author and a publisher. We can talk about this later," Rainey spoke softly so only Sara would hear what she said.

As they walked towards the cluster of female Muslims, their progress was slow. Everyone stopped and greeted them and told Rainey they were happy to see her. Sara looked around, and without being noticed by Rainey, tried her best to spot the PPD's surveillance team.

While Rainey was involved with Laila and the women in the group, Sara casually walked over to the tubs that were set out against the western wall. The tubs were filled with ice and bottles of water, sodas, and fruit juices. Several groups of men were standing nearby and hadn't seemed to notice Sara standing by the tubs. Sara busied herself looking for a cold drink and listened to a group of five men discussing Rainey.

"Can we trust her?"

"She's not Muslim. She can't be trusted!"

"She's Widad's granddaughter. She grew up in the community."

"That was many years ago."

"We should ask the imam to talk with her."

"Better she talk to the cops than to us."

"What did Brother Abdul say?"

"He thinks the imams should invite her to meet with them."

"This is better, I think."

"I do not trust her. She is one of them."

"She shouldn't be drawing any pictures."

"Ahmed says she draws pictures of criminals. That can't be wrong."

"She's not one of them, not truly. She's some kind of professor of bones."

"Look—the other one…"

Sara realized she had been noticed when the men switched to Arabic. They did not look towards her; their circle got tighter and their voices much softer. Sara pretended not to notice and walked back to where Zarinah and Rainey were now positioned next to a small podium. Zarinah clapped her hands once and very soon the discussions ceased as the people looked toward Zarinah expectantly.

"Everyone please find a chair. The food is about ready to be served, but we have a small program the children have put together on short notice. Insha'Allah it will be a fine one."

Sara sat down in the empty chair next to Rainey and watched as a group of young girls, probably not older than ten, walked up to the small podium. They looked adorable and very proud to be in the program. "What in the world are they wearing on their heads over their head scarves, Rainey? It looks like they are all wearing men's handkerchiefs?"

Rainey sat very still and smiled through the silent tears that rolled down her face. She was too choked up with emotion to speak. She just grabbed Sara's hand and squeezed it.

The oldest, or perhaps tallest of the girls stood before the microphone and greeted everyone with, "As salaam'alaykum."

"Wa 'alaykum as salaam," everyone replied at once.

The leader of the group of girls then turned towards Rainey and said, "The Hijab-Ez Friendship Group of Tempe welcomes Hijabie Rose home."

Rainey nodded her head and smiled at the girls.

Each little girl then recited a Qur'an verse they had memorized to the many praises of parents and friends. When they concluded their program, Rainey was invited to the podium to speak.

"As salaam 'alaykum." Rainey greeted everyone.

They answered with, "Wa 'alaykum as salaam."

"Thank you for making my homecoming so wonderful and for welcoming my good friend Sara as well. I thank each of you who have kept the memory of my dear grandmother alive with the love and respect I have heard from many of you this afternoon. My heart and spirit are deeply touched. I can see that the food is ready and I am so anxious to taste some of the foods I remember from my childhood. I am also quite hungry, so I'll turn this program over to Sister Zarinah, who everyone knows, made this gathering happen."

Zarinah said, "Have a seat everyone, and the Tempe Chapter of the Muslim Youth Group will be serving us today."

Next, Sara and Rainey heard the blessings said by the Muslims surrounding them. Zarinah motored over to a table with Sara and Rainey taking seats on either side of her. "You know the *big* event begins once we have eaten, don't you?" Zarinah asked Rainey.

"*Big* event?" Rainey asked, with the same emphasis on the word 'big."

"Eat up and don't talk when you get your food. The Hijab-Ez fan club will be here as quickly as they can finish eating. They will be taking you to the table in the semicircle over there, and letting you autograph their Hijab-Ez Sisters Books. I set up the chairs to keep them from crowding each other and stampeding you," Zarinah said, and began an infectious belly laugh that spread to all the sisters seated at the table.

Sara relaxed at the table and watched Rainey interact with the Hijab-Ez Fan Club. Zarinah had explained that in the book series, the friendship group of girls wore the handkerchiefs to support one of the Muslim group members who had been teased by school classmates for wearing a head scarf. She also learned that it was the book character, Islamic Rose, who came up with the idea and that Islamic Rose always had a plan for the Hijab-Ez friendship group. Sara marveled to herself that the book series had endured for over twenty years.

Rainey was back at the table after the book signing and they had been talking to the many Muslim women who stopped by to speak, when Sara heard an Arabic voice coming loud and clear from somewhere inside the mosque.

"That's the *adhan,* or call to prayer. You are both welcome to join us, but it will be fine if you want to slip away once we begin to enter the masjid for prayer."

Rainey looked over at Sara and then back at Zarinah. "I think we will slip away. Sara just got into town and I know she is tired."

"I'll call you tomorrow, sweetie," Zarinah said as she turned on her wheelchair, included Sara in her smile, and headed for the ramp leading to the large opened doors of the mosque.

Mini Murder Room

Rainey and Sara walked to the unmarked loaner car. Sara got in on the passenger side and pushed the lever to recline the seat.

Rainey sat in the driver's seat and looked over at her friend, "That wasn't so bad, was it?"

"I had a really good time. The food was fabulous…I'm stuffed. The kids were adorable. So many of them wanting you to sign as Islamic Rose…that's just amazing. And your grandmother must have been an amazing woman, too. Being remembered so many years after her death with such respect and affection and some of the stories I heard today about her…she must have been a real pistol!" Sara replied.

"She was a one-of-a-kind person, no doubt about that. I miss her each day," Rainey said softly.

"I overheard a group of five Muslim men talking about imams talking to you. I am assuming these imams are the community leaders, right?" Sara didn't wait for a response but continued, "A couple of the men don't seem so willing to trust you. One of them raised objections about the police sketch work you do. Another man said it was okay because it helped get criminals. Another said that he thought you should meet together with all the imams. Then someone noticed me standing close by, and they moved closer together and started speaking Arabic."

"Good intel, Sara. The Tempe imam approached me and asked if I'd be available for a meeting tomorrow morning. He didn't say what about, other than there were some concerns the community had, and perhaps I might be able to assist. I'm hoping he wants to talk about the serial killings, and maybe I can persuade him to convince the community to cooperate with task force investigators. If all eight imams show up tomorrow for this meeting, I won't be surprised. It can save lots of time trying to get individual appointments with them. I am still going to try to meet separately with the imams of the communities where the victims lived." Rainey started the car and headed out of the parking lot.

Sara covered her mouth to smother a yawn. "It's early to bed for me tonight."

Rainey looked over at her friend and nudged her shoulder. "Don't get to comfortable with that thought. We need to get you a suitable disguise, and I need to stop by a hardware store. We'll go to the Tempe Marketplace, the local 'shopping mall on steroids.' It's colossal and only a few blocks from the mosque."

"Rainey you know I love to shop, but remember I'm your tired friend who needs some rest."

"This won't be a shopping expedition, Sara. We are going to a sports shop to buy you a baseball cap, some very large and dark shades, and a Cardinals t-shirt so when you do go to Phoenix PD you won't be easily recognized. Driving my loaner undercover car, you can park in the back employee's parking lot."

Sara groaned and clicked the lever to the upright position. A few minutes later Rainey used the turn signal and pulled into the Tempe Marketplace.

"This place is huge," Sara's eyes glazed over as she glanced at the dozens of stores, shops, and restaurants. Sara was a clothes hound and loved to shop.

Rainey laughed at the expression on Sara's face. "When we finish our quick shopping trip, we have a lot of work waiting for us at home. As soon as we get there I'm going to install a lock on the back bedroom door and convert it into a work area for this case. I'm expecting quite a few of the women you met today to eventually pay me a visit, bring me some luscious home-cooked food, and just maybe I'll be able to talk with them about the killings. A one-on-one at the house will make them feel more comfortable. I hope they will trust me enough to talk and maybe answer some questions I have."

"That means I will need to make myself scarce during these visits?" Sara asked.

"Yes, it'd probably be best. You can hang out at the library doing research or go pester the task force at Phoenix PD. We have lots to do when we get back home. I need to check in with Sergeant Ames, and I'm sure you have to report in with DC. I'm also thinking about calling the captain and setting up a meeting."

"You are not meeting him alone, and before I've run a background on him," Sara scolded.

"Get serious, Sara. I'm fully trained and can handle myself just fine. This captain, if he really is a captain, is not going to meet with me and share anything if my librarian friend is tagging along."

"You're right...I know...but I don't like it. You may need a backup. You know the Bureau doesn't want us acting like cowboys and backup is SOP!" Sara insisted.

"Then it's up to me to insist on a public place that will allow you to be around in the vicinity, but not where he can spot you lurking," Rainey shot back.

"Sounds like a solid plan to me," Sara said, giving Rainey an impish grin. "Any good-looking and single hunks on this task force?"

Rainey answered Sara by laughing out loud. Sara was irrepressible. Her quest for finding that perfect hunk was legend in the Bureau, and she went through men like tea going through a strainer.

"Now that we've got that issue settled let's go get you a baseball cap and t-shirt."

＊ ＊ ＊

Rainey and Sara surveyed their hard work with satisfied smiles. The back bedroom was now a mini murder room. They had stopped at an office supply store after finishing up at the hardware store. Rainey purchased three folding card tables, two large cork boards, an easel with a two hundred page tablet to hang on it, pins and tacks, a box of file folders, a package of legal pads, and a package of number-two lead pencils. Sara removed the paperback novels from a bookcase, making room for a makeshift filing cabinet. One card table housed two computers: one for research, and one for communication. The other two tables were set up for examining case files and writing notes. Rainey set up a "Victims" cork board and a "Killer" corkboard.

DC Britt didn't comment when Rainey gave him a progress report by phone. He wanted a written report faxed to him by morning. That meant another hour of work for Rainey. Sara was mostly silent during Rainey's call to DC; she had little to say to Rainey as well. Rainey knew she was going to have to confront Sara sooner or later, but tonight was not the time.

Rainey's phone call to Sergeant Ames didn't turn up anything new. The task force had to be doing something, but information was not trickling down to Rainey. She wondered if Sara was getting SKTF information from DC. Tomorrow she'd confront Lieutenant Jerald and if he turned squirrely... he'd get a taste of her seldom displayed, but powerful temper. If he was stonewalling her then he'd get nothing from her about any of her meetings with the Muslim community until DC Britt made it clear that the investigation was one of mutual cooperation between agencies. Being nice just didn't cut it if the PPD wasn't sharing intel. She'd also let DC know that she was still on staff at NYU and could easily get a job with any number of other large law enforcement agencies... she'd had lots of offers.

"I'm going to bed, Rainey. You should finish that report tomorrow. It's been a very long and interesting day."

"DC wants the report first thing in the morning, I have two meetings, plus I am expecting phone calls from the women to start coming in. I'd better finish this tonight. Sleep well, Sara. I'll see ya in the morning."

Confrontation - Rainey

"Major Billings' office, Sergeant Ames speaking."

"Good morning, Sarge. I'm running a bit late…got caught in a traffic snarl on I-10," Rainey said.

"No problem, RW. Lieutenant Jerald has been hanging around because he would like to meet with you as soon as you arrive. We can go over to P&E afterwards if that's okay with you?"

"Okay. My ETA is about twenty minutes. See ya when I see ya," Rainey answered and flipped the cell phone closed.

Rainey knew the lieutenant was anxious to hear about the event at the mosque yesterday. How much she told him of her plans depended on what he had to say. "I'm going to have to call the captain and set up a meet and I'm not telling Sara. He has to know something about 1 of 10 and 2 of 10 and for some reason isn't talking to the task force… why else would he be contacting me? Could be my semi-official SKTF connection or maybe because I'm an outsider like him?" Rainey shook her head and with a small smile tipping the corners of her lips she spoke out loud, "I've got to stop thinking out loud like this. The wrong person just might overhear me!"

Rainey drove to the Phoenix PD's employee back parking lot, parked in an empty slot near the back entrance of the building, and grabbed her almost empty briefcase. She pulled the baseball cap down lower on her forehead before getting out of the car.

Sergeant Ames was waiting outside the SKTF office when Rainey stepped out of the elevator.

"Didn't recognize you, RW," the Sergeant smiled cheerfully as Rainey walked up to her.

Rainey grinned as they went through the doorway and were greeted by Lieutenant Jerald. "Morning RW. Let's sit at the table. That will be all, Sarge." The lieutenant smiled at both women. Sergeant Ames looked a little disappointed as she retraced her steps to the door and left the room. *Probably hoped to listen in*, Rainey thought to herself.

Rainey sat down at the table and looked directly at the lieutenant as he broke eye contact, lowered his gaze to the table, and shuffled some papers in front of him. She hadn't acknowledged the smile the lieutenant had given her.

He tried again, "Ah… I hope you had a good afternoon meeting old friends, yesterday? I would like to hear any of your opinions or thoughts about how you were received and if you were approached by anyone in the community about the killings…ah… did anyone volunteer anything or express any thoughts about this?"

Rainey continued to look directly at the lieutenant, but didn't respond to anything he had said. She watched as a red color slowly began creeping from his neck up into his face.

"Is there something bothering you, RW?"

"You noticed? Let me begin by stating that my name is Agent Rainey Walker. You and the task force, and your boss can address me as Agent Walker or as Rainey. I don't play games when people's lives are at stake and I don't like to be jerked around by you, your boss, or even my boss. My contribution to this task force is going to be dictated by me, Lieutenant Jerald. It is my skills, my knowledge, and in this instance, my access to the Muslim community that was offered by me to the task force right in this room two days ago. I was honest and upfront."

"Agent Walker…Rainey…no one is jerking you around that I know of…" Lieutenant Jerald protested.

"Asking me how the event went yesterday when you had a team of six SKTF running surveillance cameras and at least two task force members dressed as Muslims and milling around listening in on discussions while never mentioning this to me two days ago?"

"We had our reasons…"

"I don't even want to go there," Rainey said in a tone of voice that brooked no argument from the lieutenant. "Let's talk about the copied case files I was given, or maybe we should talk about what was left out of those files? Maybe we can talk about 1 of 10 and 2 of 10 and why their information is missing from the Victim's Board?"

"Rainey, there is much more to this investigation…you nailed it. We haven't given you all the intel we have. There are reasons for this, and I am not authorized to explain those reasons to you. Can't you trust me, the task force members you met, my boss, and your boss, not to do anything that would compromise this investigation and you personally?"

"You want me to operate on partial intel, maybe betray confidences given from people who have treated me with kindness all my life, and cash in on their respect and love for my grandmother? You want me to give the task force whatever information I can acquire and that's it?" Rainey's voice was soft, her demeanor calm, and her words laden with steel…each one precisely bitten off and filling the space between her and the lieutenant with her unspoken anger. Her eyes flashed and bored into Lieutenant Jerald as she waited for him to respond.

"All I can tell you is there are national security concerns and…"

"That's BS and you know it," Rainey said without raising her voice. Rainey decided against mentioning the captain. If national security was somehow implicated in this case, Rainey knew there was no way she would be getting any information out of the lieutenant or Major Billings.

"I think this meeting is over, Lieutenant Jerald. I gave a copy of my report to Sergeant Ames with a schedule of meetings I have set up. If I learn anything, or members of the community are willing to talk with the task force, I'll call Sergeant Ames or fax in a report."

Lieutenant Jerald remained seated as Rainey stood and picked up her briefcase. He lowered his eyes as Rainey paused and briefly stared at him. "You wasted a good asset by shutting me out, Lieutenant Jerald. You'll get what information I can from the community. Don't call me, I'll call you."

Rainey closed the door quietly behind her and saw Sergeant Ames just outside the door waiting around to take her to P&E. Sergeant Ames was startled when Rainey came through the SKTF door. She thought Rainey would be in the briefing for at least an hour. The sergeant tried to hide the paperback book she had been reading in the slit between the buttons of her uniform shirt, but it dropped to the floor.

Rainey looked down at the book. "I hope you enjoyed my grandmother's series. Book Two is my personal favorite." The sergeant's face was a flaming red as she picked up the book and then looked up at Rainey.

Before she could say anything, Rainey said in a voice that lacked its usual friendliness, "Let's get over to P&E, now. I have meetings scheduled and need to get this done first." Rainey strode to the elevator at the end of the hallway with the Sergeant hurrying to catch up.

The P&E reports were accurate. Looking at the evidence from each of the killings, Rainey was struck by just how little there was.

The deep and jagged rending of each of the scarves imprinted on Rainey's heart. They were dealing with a smart and vicious criminal psycho.

As soon as Rainey pulled out of the parking lot and left Phoenix headquarters she found a place to pull over on a quiet street and park. She took the business card the captain had given her out of her wallet and dialed the number. Two rings and a voice message told Rainey to leave a first name, call back phone number and she would be contacted. Rainey was disappointed. She wanted to set up a meeting now before her meeting with the imam in Tempe.

Next she opened the phone to speed dial Sara. It was time for Rainey to confront her friend. If Sara stonewalled her or worse, lied to her, Rainey would be devastated.

The Killer

The day after the Muslim event at the Tempe mosque, the killer was up early and preparing to leave for the breakfast meeting with that idiot from the Phoenix PD. The killer was still enraged to the point where even fondling the swatches of hair failed to bring calm to chaotic thoughts. Six of 10 had been at the community event and the killer had intended to watch her every move, but was distracted by the SKTF surveillance crew and those two women. Who were they? They weren't Muslim. The killer's anger had mounted as any opportunity of mingling in the Muslim crowd or getting in close enough to 6 of 10 was thwarted by the cameras of the task force.

Instead the killer had followed the two women once they left the event and watched as they shopped. The killer remembered the tall one jogging in the park and waving.

Suddenly the killer's mouth twisted into a contemptuous sneer remembering the tall one and her friendly smile as she passed by in the hardware store aisle. The short one, up close, was much younger than she first appeared to be, even with that grey hair and those ugly wire glasses. The killer's animal-like instincts had gone on high alert. The two women in the long skirts acting so chummy with those heathens were more than what they appeared to be. The killer followed them home and filed away the address for the future. They wouldn't be hard to find and if they got in the way...then they'd become collateral damage.

This mission was going to be finished, and no one was going to stop it! It was almost time to meet the idiot for breakfast and find out what new information he had about the investigation. Maybe that pig would know something. He would be collateral damage in the near future.

The face in the mirror reflected a fierce image filled with a determination that the task force was going to find it difficult to stop.

The Captain

Before Rainey could depress Sara's number her phone rang. "Hey, Rainey, briefing finished? Learn anything else from P&E? What did the lieutenant think about you having a meeting this afternoon with the Muslim leaders? Do you have time to meet someplace before your meeting at the mosque?"

Rainey waited impatiently for Sara to wind down with the questions. Just then her disposable cell phone rang. "Hold on, Sara. I got a call on the other phone. I'll call you back."

"Agent Walker?" the smooth voice of the captain asked.

"Yes. I called because I want to meet. The sooner the better," Rainey said hurriedly before he could say anything else.

"I can meet you at that Mexican restaurant. How soon can you get there?"

"I'll be there in thirty minutes if I don't get caught in another traffic jam. I'm leaving downtown Phoenix," Rainey replied.

"See you in thirty," the phone clicked dead. *Now there's no turning back*, Rainey thought. Rainey went over the situation in her thoughts and planned her approach. The restaurant would be safe enough and they'd be in broad daylight. She'd be careful where she parked and make sure she left the meeting before the captain did. She'd insist they sit by a window, if he arrived first, and she'd insist he remain seated where she could watch him as she left the restaurant and got in her car.

Rainey speed dialed Sara. Before Sara could say a word, Rainey said, "I left my briefcase back at the PD. No time to meet up if I want to get to my meeting on time. See you back at the house later." Rainey hung up and switched the phone to voice messaging. Sara would be ticked off and know something was going on, but there was nothing she could do. She'd have to wait it out until Rainey called or returned to the house later. Rainey had home field advantage and a car. Sara was a fish out of water.

Rainey fastened her ankle holster and 5-shot Chief's Special revolver to her leg, then carefully rolled her pant leg down. She fished around the briefcase, finding two full speed loaders which she jammed into her right front jeans pocket. She was ready to meet the captain. Rainey drove eastbound on I-10, breaking every speed limit. She wanted to arrive at the restaurant before the captain.

Rainey silently rehearsed the questions she wanted to put to the captain. Would he stonewall her? What information was he looking for? Was he on-duty or assignment? Was he even a captain in the Army? *Call me when you need my help…*the cryptic message repeated itself in Rainey's thoughts as she also thought about him and the meeting. How much will I tell him? "Depends on how much he's willing to tell me," she thought out loud.

Rainey approached the restaurant from the back and drove slowly looking at the vehicles and plates…looking for rental cars or out of state plates. Nothing. She drove past the restaurant once. He wasn't waiting outside at one of the outdoor tables. She scanned the cars in the parking lot and didn't see him waiting in any of the cars. She parked her car in a slot close to the restaurant entrance, got out, and clicked the locks on the doors.

Inside the temperature was cool and comfortable. Only a few couples with kids in tow. She'd arrived first. Rainey let out a small sigh that lowered her anxiety level, but didn't remove it completely.

She walked to a corner table by one of the two front windows, and sat down with her back to a wall and facing the entrance door.

At exactly thirty minutes from the time the captain hung up, Rainey saw him crossing the parking lot. She didn't see him drive up or park. "Damn," she said under her breath. She'd lost her chance to see what he was driving.

The captain gave Rainey a mega-watt smile and said, "Agent Walker," as he pulled out a chair and sat opposite her.

"Captain," Rainey answered.

The waitress hurried over with menus. The captain waved the menus away and said, "We'll have iced tea now and I'll signal you when we decide if we want to order something else. The waitress returned in a few minutes and practically stumbled when the captain smiled his thanks.

"How can I help you," were the next words out of the captain's mouth.

"You can begin by showing me some official and credible identification. Next you can tell me if you approached me officially or unofficially, third you can tell me what you know about 1 of 10 and 2 of 10, and lastly you can help me by telling me what you want from me," Rainey said without taking her eyes off the captain's face. He was good. No show of surprise, emotion… nada. He sat there passively and gave away nothing: no tensing of muscles, no looking away or downward…no throat clearing, no fidgeting. His hands lay palms down on the top of the table. Rainey could not begin to guess what he was thinking or gauge what his responses would be. But boy, he was one beautiful hunk of manhood.

"If I may?" the captain indicated he intended to take something out of his back pant pocket. Rainey nodded an okay. He was so smooth.

The captain slid his ID wallet across the table to Rainey. She opened it and looked it over carefully. "So why did you give me the business card the other day? Why didn't you just hand me your ID like today?"

"I didn't know the other day who that middle-aged woman with you was and I wanted time to check her out. I didn't want to talk business in front of her," he grinned and accepted his ID wallet back. "Finding out your best friend, FBI Agent Sara James is on vacation leave…remove the wig, granny glasses, and 3-inch heels, and who else would be visiting you while you are officially on vacation?"

Rainey's respect for the captain went up a half notch.

"I'm on vacation leave, too. Can we dispense with the formalities and move to first name basis? I'm Jonathan, Jonah to my friends, and you are Rainey. Nice to meet you, Rainey." His megawatt smile flashed again.

Rainey nodded assent again and tossed the ball back to him, "Is your vacation official or unofficial?"

"Before I answer that and your 1 of 10 and 2 of 10 questions, I need to tell you something," Jonah said. "Can you just listen for a bit?'

"Okay," Rainey said, and took a long sip of her iced tea.

"In the US Army I am assigned to I-SID. Do you know what the I-SID is or does for the Army?"

Rainey shook her head no.

"I-SID is the International Special Investigations Division. We work only major crimes involving military personnel and the crimes must be international in nature. Following me?"

"Yes."

"Sometimes I-SID officers are assigned or loaned out to other agencies. Something like you being employed by the FBI, but you are also loaned out to other law enforcement agencies as a consultant, right?"

"Right." Rainey was intrigued and wondering where the captain was headed. She wasn't quite ready to think of him as Jonah, yet.

"You could say that I am on vacation from I-SID officially, but unofficially on loan to another agency, an international agency."

"But you are not at liberty to tell me which agency because it's on a need to know basis, right?" Rainey said, with a shade of sarcasm. Lieutenant Jerald's similar excuse for withholding intel just a few short hours ago still had Rainey steamed.

"Is that what you were told when you asked about 1 of 10 and 2 of 10 at Phoenix headquarters? Was it Major Billings or that ass, Lieutenant Jerald, who whipped that on you?"

Rainey stared him and waited. Jonah could see she was getting mulish and her patience was wearing thin.

"I'd like to tell you a hypothetical story and hope I can count on just about 10 more minutes of your time. I know you have a meeting to go to and I won't hold you up. Can I have 10 more minutes, Rainey?"

Rainey nodded. *If he only knew. Wild horses couldn't drag me away from this table!* Jonah had her hooked and she wasn't budging until he told his story.

"A high ranking government official was put in charge of an investigation of two homicides in two different countries. The killer profile and method of killing pointed to an international serial killer, and the possible suspects were thought to be among a group of current and prior military personnel. Several years later, three new victims turn up in the USA in the same state, and the victims are living within twenty miles of each other. The killer profile and method of killing are almost identical to the first two murders."

Jonah paused to take a long drink of his tea while keeping his eyes focused on Rainey. He watched the dawning comprehension flood Rainey's face.

"Now just suppose this high ranking government official sent a buffoon slash high ranking military investigator, looking for a brass ring to promotion, to the local law enforcement agency investigating the three state-side murders. This investigator's job was to get intel without giving any and to put a lid on things so the government and military would not be embarrassed. And suppose he showed up and the first words out of his mouth were 'Homeland Security, national security situation. Need to know only'?

"The story is that the local law enforcement agency got its feathers ruffled, words like stealing thunder and taking credit were part of a shouting match. Now we all know that in situations like this, the brass gets involved, and both the military investigator and the local law enforcement officials were told to play nice. The result being, both agencies bent over backwards not to cooperate, but on the surface acted as if they were knocking themselves out to get along. Does this sound like a familiar story to you, Rainey?"

"I've heard similar stories," Rainey said with a calmness she didn't feel. "Is there more to this story?"

"If you can spare me a few more minutes, I'll get to the part you'll really appreciate," Jonah said, following with his mega-watt smile that now was making Rainey's toes curl.

Rainey pretended to check the time on her wrist watch and then nodded and said, "I have a few more minutes, Jonah."

"A week or so later a major at this same local law enforcement agency gets a phone call from an alma mater brother who happens to be a big shot working in the Profilers Division of the FBI. This FBI guy tells his friend he's been tracking the serial killings in the press and such, and he thinks he might be able to offer some help. The major is immediately suspicious. The FBI is legendary for butting into local high profile cases and stealing glory from local law enforcement." Jonah grins impishly at Rainey. She can't help herself and laughs.

"The FBI guy says he knows his buddy's troops are having problems dealing with the Muslim community because the Muslims don't trust cops. He tells his buddy he can loan him a person who will be welcomed into the community...one of the agents working under his command. He tells the major this agent can work as a consultant to the task force because she can gain access and cooperation from the Muslim community. The major and the FBI make a deal to work together, but the major plans to limit the FBI consultant's access to the case, use her then send her packing. Knowing his consultant will be none too happy with an assignment while supposedly on vacation, this FBI guy sends another agent to babysit and to act as his snitch.

"We have a consultant who is, on the surface, treated friendly by the local law enforcement and a boss with his own agenda, a friend sent to watch and report to the FBI guy, and then along comes a smooth talking guy who follows the consultant around until she has to notice him and find out what he wants." Jonah paused and drained the last of his tea from the glass.

"And is this smooth talking guy going to tell the consultant what he wants and why he has been *stalking* the consultant?" Rainey asks sweetly, with eyes alight with humor.

"This smooth talking guy decides to take the consultant out to dinner after an important meeting and explain what the 1 of 10 and 2 of 10 connections are to the serial killings."

Rainey looked at her wrist watch this time to really check the time. "Jonah, if I don't leave now I'll be late and being late is viewed as very bad manners. Can I call you after the meeting? I need to get home and have a small discussion with my snitch, and I don't intend for her to join us for dinner."

"Sure. Just call that number on the card. I'll pay for the tea. You get a move on," Jonah said. He didn't have to repeat himself. Rainey was already standing and walked quickly away. She turned at the door to give Jonah a small salute.

Meeting at the Masjid

Rainey slowed and turned her car into the driveway. The lights were on in the murder room. *Sara must be working,* Rainey thought, and turned off the ignition. She dreaded what she had decided to do about Sara. With any luck at all she'd pull it off and maybe, just maybe, when this case was over, she and Sara would be able to talk about things openly and honestly.

Rainey leaned her head back against the head rest, closed her eyes, and thought about the meeting at the mosque. She was surprised when the meeting was nothing like she had expected it to be. As Grams might say if she were here, *Thank God for Sister Zarinah!*

Arriving at the mosque, Rainey saw Zarinah's familiar self seated in her wheelchair waiting on the walkway to the mosque's front doors. After giving salaams, Zarinah told her that they would be meeting the Tempe imam in his office. She quickly explained that out of courtesy to Rainey and for everyone's benefit, Zarinah had been invited to attend the meeting. Rainey remembered the Islamic teaching about men and women who are not blood relatives not meeting one-on-one alone. Islam teaches that this convention is for the good of both the male and female… to reduce any possibility of improper conduct. Rainey thought of her physical attraction to the captain and acknowledged a better understanding of this Islamic practice.

Inside the office, the imam had been cordial. He explained that the other community leaders would be setting up appointments with Rainey. They had asked him to meet with her first to set up some ground rules. Rainey wasn't expecting the typed copy the imam slid across the desk to her.

Rainey opened her eyes and glanced down at the passenger seat where she had placed the list. She picked it up and re-read it:

As Salaam'Alaykum,

The imams of the eight Muslim communities in Maricopa County, Arizona met and have each agreed to the listed ground rules for assisting with the investigations into the deaths of three Muslim women in our communities:

1. *Meetings between Agent Rainey Walker and each community leader will be conducted at each community leader's masjid office.*

2. *Present at each of these meetings will be Agent Walker, Sister Zarinah Awad, and the imam.*

3. *At the masjid communities where a member sister was killed, adult family members may also be present at the meetings.*

4. *Agent Walker may not record the meetings, but she may take written notes.*

5. *Each imam who meets with Agent Walker will give her a list of their masjid community members.*

6. *Only adult members choosing to be contacted individually by Agent Walker will be listed on a separate contact list.*

7. *Agent Walker will be invited to speak at the Tempe masjid after the Friday prayer. Agent Walker may*

> bring any written information concerning the safety
> of Muslim communities and information about the
> ongoing police cases affecting the Muslim communities.
> Copies of this information will be distributed to those
> attending this meeting.

8. Agent Walker may share the information provided with
   the Phoenix Police Department.

9. Sister Zarinah Awad has agreed to attend any meetings
   and provide any translation assistance that could be
   needed.

10. No other law enforcement officials will be invited to the
    scheduled meetings.

Rainey understood the mistrust the communities had with
law enforcement. It had accumulated over a period of a decade
or more. Rainey realized that the imams and some of the community members realized that their cooperation was necessary to
progress in the investigations...but the Muslims were scared. The
men knew their wives, sisters, and daughters were the targets of a
vicious killer and their first reaction was to try to isolate and protect the women in the communities. Rainey had noted the armed
private security at the community event the day before and had
not commented about this, even to Zarinah, as everyone seemed
to have chosen not to acknowledge their presence.

Rainey sighed deeply. She hoped this compromise by the
Muslim community would be sufficient for the local police. They
were not going to be happy about the limitations and exclusions.
Rainey only hoped the task force, especially some of the cowboys,
didn't initiate any action that would damage these first steps in
building some trust and lines of communications with the Muslim communities.

Sara's reaction would be typical for Sara. She'd rant and rave
and then cool down. DC Britt wouldn't like it either that his spy

wouldn't be getting first hand information, but would have to rely on Rainey. No, Sara wouldn't like it one bit having to stay at home doing the grunt work. Rainey felt a grin spreading across her face. *Serves her right*, she thought for the second time in a couple days.

Rainey glanced up and saw Sara standing in the opened doorway with her palms turned up indicating the question, "What's up?" Rainey gathered her briefcase, purse and the ground rules list and got out of the car...ready to face one of Sara's famous rants.

Confrontation – Sara

"I thought you must have fallen asleep in the car. What were you doing just sitting there? How did the meeting go? Did all the imams show up?" Sara paused to catch her breath before she could start the next barrage of questions.

"If you step aside and let me by, I'll answer your questions, but only after I change clothes. You can fix me a tall glass of tea while I'm doing that," Rainey answered, and softened her words by giving Sara a quick hug.

"Thanks!" Rainey said as she sat in her grandmother's old recliner. Sara sat opposite Rainey on the couch and was trying hard to keep her mouth shut and let Rainey speak before she asked more questions.

But Sara couldn't help herself. Being cooped up all day, at the library first, and then waiting hours for Rainey to return home, Sara was moody and on a short fuse. She just couldn't keep quiet.

"I've been sitting around all day by myself…totally shut out from all that's going on. DC called me twice and is none too happy. Said you haven't called him or sent in any new reports!" Sara gave Rainey an aggrieved look.

"Well my dearest best friend," Rainey paused, "You've been reporting in regularly to the boss. I figured you were telling him what he needed to know and you've been receiving all the intel he's been keeping from me." Rainey's sugary-sweet reply was laced with sarcasm.

"I don't know what you mean by that crack," Sara sputtered as her face flushed brick red.

"You knew about the task force surveillance yesterday. You also knew about Homeland Security and the Phoenix PD having a confrontation about sharing information and jurisdictional issues," Rainey said with smug satisfaction as she saw Sara's mouth drop open.

"How did you learn about all that?" Sara said softly, confirming what Jonah told Rainey. Her boss and the task force were limiting the information they were sharing with her, and Sara knew this all along and kept quiet. Either they thought she was not fit to have access or they distrusted her ties to the Muslim community, even though they expected her to exploit those ties.

Rainey decided, while staring at Sara's face with the dismay and guilt clearly written on it, that she would keep Sara ignorant about her past and future meetings with Jonah. Rainey didn't want Sara tagging along later that evening when Rainey met him again. She'd tell Sara she was invited to a Muslim home and there wouldn't be any discussion about the killings…just a social invitation extended only to Rainey. She had had misgivings at the mosque about agreeing that the authorities be excluded from her meetings with the imams, but now she was glad they had been excluded and it was in writing. DC Britt, Lieutenant Jerald, and Major Billings could not accuse Rainey of trying to keep them out.

"You're not going to tell me, are you?" Sara said quietly.

Rainey did not answer. Instead, she handed Sara the typed list of ground rules, and waited while Sara read the content.

"What am I supposed to be doing while you go to these meetings?" Sara asked. Rainey could see she was not happy about the rules.

"You can type up my notes into reports you can send the boss. You can take copies of the reports to the task force and discuss whatever it is they want to discuss with you. You are the field agent and liaison to DC, not me. I am just a consultant on vacation doing my small bit to help form a communications bridge between the Muslim community and the task force. I suggest you call Sergeant Ames and Lieutenant Jerald, with whom I have no doubt you have already made contact on your own, and arrange to get me the information the task force would like the Muslim communities to have. You could even see to it that copies are made so I can leave them at the mosque for distribution. I am sure the boss will give you additional work or assignments as he sees fit."

"You can't just bow out of the investigation like this!" Sara angrily exclaimed.

"I am not bowing out. I am going to do what I was asked to do—talk to Muslims in the communities and ask them to cooperate with the task force and FBI. I'll gather information from the Muslims willing to meet with me and document what might be helpful. I'll pass it on to the task force and our boss through you. Other than that, I am on vacation and intend to relax and enjoy myself."

Sara stood up and began pacing in front of Rainey. "I told DC that this was a bad idea…keeping you in the dark and treating you with kid gloves. He wouldn't listen and then that ass, Lieutenant Jerald, kept insisting your ties to the community might color your judgment! That really ticked me off. You haven't lived in your hometown in almost a decade…I am so…" Sara didn't finish what she was going to say. She stopped pacing and stood in front of Rainey and asked, "You're serious, aren't you?"

"Absolutely, Sara. I know you have a job to do. If you feel uncomfortable staying here, I won't be offended if you want to get a hotel room downtown. You are welcome to stay here, but I will be watching to see who is dogging me if you or DC decide to do that."

"You know this could cost you your job, Rainey, if DC thinks you are not willing to do the work you are assigned and cooperate with everyone?"

"But I am co-operating and doing what I was asked by the task force and instructed to do by DC. Because I am not an imbecile and figured out that all of you were jerking me around... well, I think DC would have a tough time terminating me based on what all of you did and not what I failed to do."

Sara went back to the couch and sat down. It was obvious she didn't have anything to say in response to Rainey's assessment of the situation.

"All these games make me sick," Rainey said softly. "Three women have been brutally killed and mutilated, with probably two other murders...maybe you know something about that and haven't shared it with me...I do know that this serial killer intends to kill five more Muslim women.

"Two police agencies, maybe three, are trying to get one up on the others, and with me. I'm telling you so you can report to DC...I am not playing games with five more women's lives at risk. There is a killer out there waiting for an opportunity to strike again. I know you were doing your job, Sara, but I just didn't expect you to lie to me."

Rainey got up and walked into the dining room. She opened her briefcase on the table and withdrew a notepad. She walked back into the living room and placed the notepad on the coffee table in front of Sara. "Here are my notes on the meeting with Lieutenant Jerald this morning and my notes on the meeting at the Tempe mosque this afternoon. I'm going to take a shower. I've been invited to an old friend's house for dinner. There's plenty of food in the fridge or you can call out for a pizza and salad."

Sara didn't look up or respond. She just sat on the couch and watched as Rainey walked down the hallway towards her bedroom. A feeling of dread crept over Sara. She had to call DC and depending on what he said, call Lieutenant Jerald. Neither was going to be happy.

About thirty minutes later Rainey entered the living room. Sara was still sitting on the couch. "Tomorrow I'll rent a car from Enterprise and give you the keys to the loaner car from Phoenix PD. You'll need a car to get around and go to meetings and such with the task force." Rainey said.

Sara just nodded her head. "What about the plan to set up a meeting with that captain? I used every contact I know and came up with zilch on him today," Sara asked.

Rainey paused at the open front door. "Why not ask for some help from DC or Lieutenant Jerald? If he contacts me again, I'll tell him he needs to talk to you...the FBI field agent assigned to the SKTF. I have no interest in getting involved with an unknown and have too much to do with interviewing Muslims to play silly games with some jerk."

Sara stared at the closed door. Should she stay here with Rainey or get a hotel room? Sara shrugged. DC Britt would be making that decision and he was waiting for her call.

Rainey flipped the cover of her disposable phone and dialed Jonah. Two rings and a voice message told her to leave a first name, call back phone number, and she would be contacted. Within seconds Rainey's phone rang.

"Hi, Rainey, it was getting late and I thought you had changed your mind?" Jonah said when Rainey answered his call back.

"Hi Jonah. The meeting at the mosque ended earlier than I thought, but my discussion with my friend lasted much longer. I'll explain when we meet. I know a quite café just south of Tempe. Actually it's on the Yaqui reservation. Go south on Priest past Southern and about ½ mile you'll see Rosita's on your left. If you can, park out front. If you have to park in back, your car might just get spray painted."

Jonah chuckled. "A rough neighborhood?"

"Not really. The teens there are famous for their graffiti art. Have been generation after generation and they have been known to use a car or two as a landscape," Rainey replied.

"See you in about twenty," Jonah said and broke the connection.

Rainey was already seated at a corner table, back to the wall, and looking out the window at Jonah as he got out of his car and started towards the front door of Rosita's. He was dressed in a blue plaid cowboy shirt with pearlized snaps for buttons at the shirt front and cuffs, Wrangler jeans, hand-tooled leather boots, and a modified Stetson on his head. Jonah was dressed like a typical southwestern cowboy meeting a date for dinner. He fit right in with the other male diners. Jonah removed the Stetson as he walked toward the table where Rainey was seated.

"Evening, Rainey," Jonah said, as he tossed the Stetson carelessly on an empty chair to Rainey's right. He pulled out the chair opposite Rainey and eased his tall, muscular frame into the chair.

"Jonah, I took the liberty of ordering. I hope you don't mind. It'll save time and interruptions," Rainey said quickly to cover her nervousness.

"No problem." Jonah said as he placed his hands on the table and waited for Rainey to begin. *She looks beautiful tonight, but worried. I love the way her brow creases when she concentrates.* Rainey was dressed in a casual long grey skirt and an emerald green soft pullover that matched the color of her eyes perfectly. *I don't think she even knows how beautiful she is,* Jonah thought, watching her fingers as she unconsciously shredded a paper napkin. Their waitress brought two steaming platters of spaghetti and meatballs and two Caesar salads to the table. "We have a great house wine," she said to Rainey and glanced shyly at Jonah.

"I'll stick with the iced tea for now. Jonah?"

"Iced tea is fine, but I'd like a black coffee once we finish our meal, please." He turned his smile on the young waitress and she stammered an okay and nearly dropped her serving tray.

"Do women always stutter and drop things around you?" Rainey teased Jonah. The waitress' obvious attraction to Jonah and almost losing the serving tray seemed to break the nervous tension that kept Rainey from feeling at ease with Jonah.

Jonah's embarrassed laugh and the sheepish look on his face told Rainey that he was very aware of the power of his smile. She'd have to watch herself and make sure he didn't get any ideas about that smile of his having any effect on her.

"Let's not talk shop until after we eat," Rainey suggested.

Jonah nodded his agreement. They spent a companionable hour eating and did very little talking.

Rainey put her fork down on her empty plate and licked a dab of sauce off her right finger.

"Delicious. I'm stuffed."

Jonah had finished a few minutes before her and was savoring his mug of coffee. "That was the best spaghetti and meatballs I've ever eaten. Thanks for ordering and inviting me here," Jonah said as he put his mug on the table.

"When I was a kid this was a favorite place of mine and my grandmother's. The owner's daughter, Christina, and I went to school together. Our waitress is her daughter."

"I'd like to go to my office and talk, but wasn't sure if you would feel comfortable with that," Jonah said, changing the subject. "I didn't want to carry around my laptop or files and then have to leave everything in my car. I had thought that if it would be okay with you I could take you there and when we were finished I'd drive you back here? Or maybe you would prefer to follow me there in your own car, but I didn't see your car parked out front when I arrived?"

"My car is parked in the rear employee's parking lot. No one would dare spray paint it. Rosita would break their neck," Rainey said, and grinned as Jonah laughed out loud. "I think I'd rather follow you. Just give me directions in case we get separated by traffic. I didn't bring any files with me either for the same reasons."

After giving Rainey his office location he asked, "Are you familiar with that part of Phoenix?"

"It's right across from the Phoenix PD," Rainey said, and her estimation of Jonah's resourcefulness went up a notch. "Office space in that building and at that location is a premium," she remarked.

"Don't I know it! I'm just glad I'm not paying the temporary rent. It's on a short-term lease."

"I'm going to the powder room and will go out the back way through the kitchen. I'll meet you in the parking garage under the building in about thirty minutes. I'll wait there until I see you in case we get separated."

Jonah picked up the check left by the young waitress. He extracted two twenties from his billfold and left them on the table. On his way to the front door he stopped the waitress and handed her a $10. "Thanks for the great service. Please tell the cook that I enjoyed the meal. The meatballs were the best I've ever eaten."

The young waitress murmured, "Gracias," and smiled at Jonah before he turned and left the restaurant.

Jonah was standing next to the driver's door of his parked car as Rainey drove in and parked next to him. As Rainey got out of her vehicle, he smiled at her. "I think it's time for us to get down to work." They took the elevator to the second floor and when it stopped they walked about half way down the hall way of closed office doors before Jonah stopped at Room 518, inserted a key card, and then punched some numbers on a key pad. He then placed his thumb on the key pad. Rainey heard several locks disengage. Jonah turned to Rainey, "Can't be too careful."

Rainey was curious. "What would happen if someone tried to break into your office?"

Jonah unsmilingly looked at her and seemed to be measuring his words carefully before he spoke. "That individual would get a very unpleasant surprise." Jonah turned the door knob and opened the door, but paused. "When I close the door behind us the locking mechanism will engage. Opening the door is activated by a voice activated code word. He held up the key card. When I depress the right corner I say the code word. When I get ready to leave I depress the key card again, say the word, and the door opens."

Rainey hesitated at the threshold of the open doorway. She wasn't about to get locked into a room with Jonah. She didn't trust him that much. Jonah saw her hesitation. He said," I'll have you say your name as the code word. You can go inside and shut the door. Then depress the key card here, and say Rainey and the door will open. You can keep the key card with you while we are in the room. Will that work for you?"

Rainey took the key card from Jonah, depressed the left corner and spoke her name. Jonah hit the light switch when the door opened. She went into the office and shut the door. She quickly glanced around the room. She noted an expensive looking equipment setup by the opaque window facing the Phoenix headquarters, a small gray metal office desk with nothing on it but a blotter, and two office chairs. To the right of the equipment she noticed a door with another keypad on it. No door knob was visible. Not wanting Jonah to think she was snooping, she depressed the key card, said her name, and heard the door locks click and watched as the door opened slightly. Jonah pushed the door open and smiled at her. "Okay?"

Rainey nodded and slipped the key card into a pocket in her skirt. "Okay." she smiled back at him.

Jonah walked over to the wall, keyed in some numbers and again used his thumb to open a closet. The door opened and Jonah took out a laptop and a large expandable folder bulging with files and placed both on his desk. He watched as Rainey looked over the electronics facing the window. "Have a seat, Rainey and I'll explain later about that equipment behind us." Rainey sat down in the chair next to his and watched as he powered up his computer and then clicked on a folder titled "1 of 10."

"Before you read the first file I'd like to provide you some background information." Rainey dragged her eyes away from the computer screen and looked expectantly at Jonah.

"Can I make some notes on the file content?" Rainey asked.

Jonah reached into the expandable folder and selected a slim file. "I've typed up the relevant facts for you. If you want to skim through them and add anything to them, you can," replied Jonah. "But first, the background information, okay?"

Rainey nodded giving her full attention to Jonah.

"The killer the FBI and Phoenix PD call the Scarf Killer became active about two years ago, as far as Interpol knows."

"Interpol," Rainey stated with a raised eyebrow.

"I showed you my identification. I am a US Army captain and I am assigned to I-SID, but I am also on temporary loan to Interpol. I am here in Phoenix working undercover as an Interpol agent. I have been tracking the Ten-Count Killer for about a year. The Ten-Count Killer has the same MO as your Scarf Killer. We are almost certain they are the same killer."

"What makes your agency think so?" Rainey's voice trailed off as dawning comprehension crossed her face. "1 of 10 and 2 of 10…your killer left Post-it notes on the victims necks and mutilated their faces…the victims are female Muslims?"

"Correct, Rainey. Interpol is involved because the first victim was killed in Iraq and about a year later the second victim was killed in Bosnia. The trail went cold for about six months. I was in Europe when I received intel about the first two killings here in Arizona. We didn't have any information about whether the killer was leaving Post-it notes on the victims, but everything else in the news and the killer profile sent to law enforcement agencies was similar. Interpol contacted SID and the Army sent another SID agent to talk to officials running the SK task force. They sent an idiot who botched everything. He ticked off the Phoenix brass… tried to throw his weight around by spouting the 'national security, need-to-know basis' crap. He got shown the door. I can't say as I blame PPD. It took me a week to get things in order in Europe and by the time I got to Phoenix there had been a third killing."

"So that equipment does…listens in on the task force?" Rainey looked at Jonah disapprovingly.

"I'll get to the reason for it soon. My bosses thought it best not to make another approach with Phoenix PD and the task force until we could confirm whether the Scarf Killer is our Ten-Count Killer," Jonah stated, meeting Rainey's eyes.

"And following me and making it obvious? What was that all about?" Rainey asked.

"I was told that you would be here in Arizona and assigned to work with the task force because of your connections with the Muslim community. My boss thought my boyish good looks and charming smile might intrigue you," he said sheepishly. "My boss got some wrong intel. He didn't know you're a straight arrow."

Rainey thought about what Jonah said and realized that maybe his boss had confused her with Sara. Not by their looks, but by Sara's reputation in the agency as a man hunter. It didn't matter now. *What is important is the linkage between the Ten-Count Killer and the Scarf Killer,* she thought to herself. Rainey needed more information about the Ten-Count Killer's victims and why the US Army was involved. Interpol involvement was understandable as the serial killer was operating internationally in three countries.

"Before I talk to you about the Scarf Killer, Jonah, tell me why the Army is involved."

Jonah hesitated and turned his compelling gaze to a point beyond Rainey's right shoulder. Rainey waited.

"I am authorized to contact you and get as much information as possible from you and share as little information as possible," Jonah stated matter-of-factly. He did not flinch as he watched the anger flash in her emerald eyes. "By getting close to you, it was hoped I'd get close to the task force investigation and to the Muslim community."

"So… you thought honesty would do the trick?" Rainey's words were cold, like icicles, as she stared at Jonah.

"I sat in this room for days photographing every single woman entering the Phoenix headquarters waiting for you to show up and then I followed you and tried the smile and intrigue ploy on you. I got nowhere and was glad! I realized the intel I had was all wrong. I was and am sincere when I wrote on that business card to call me when you needed help. My boss sent word that you were being used by the task force to gather information, but were not being completely kept up to date with task force activities and information. The task force decision to only use you to gather intel from the Muslim community, is in my opinion, a big mistake."

"The picture taking?" Rainey asked.

"I didn't have a recent photograph of you and didn't know when you would be arriving in Arizona and if you would agree to work on your vacation. Your pictures on SID file are prior to your becoming employed with the FBI. I had no idea what you looked like now. I took photos of women with your height, coloring etc. going into the Phoenix PD and processed them. I sent them to a friend who has the capabilities of accessing files that have a more recent photo of you. Don't ask." That was one piece of information Jonah would not be sharing with Rainey.

Rainey knew Jonah wasn't going to tell her anything more about his source. She had sources too, and didn't share them, not even with Sara. She thought his explanation about the expensive equipment pointed at the Phoenix headquarters was flimsy, but decided to let it pass for the moment or until she learned more about what Jonah was up to.

"Are you ready to confirm for me whether the three victims of the *Scarf Killer* were killed by the Ten-Count Killer? If I get a yes confirmation from you, I'll share why the US Army SID is involved."

Rainey breathed deeply, and made a decision she hoped was the right one. "Each of the three victims had a yellow Post-it note placed under the chin on the neck. The text on the first victim Post-it was 3 of 10, the second victim text was 4 of 10, and the third victim text was 5 of 10. The killings are coming closer in time and everyone is extremely concerned that there is little evidence and no leads. The task force didn't share any information in the copies of the files they gave me about 1 of 10 or 2 of 10. I don't know what information they have, if any. What they are concerned with is catching the killer before there is a 6 of 10 victim."

"Even after three killings, the Muslim community is still not cooperating with the task force?" Jonah asked.

"The problem is how the community was initially approached and the lack of understanding about Islamic beliefs and practices which resulted in their becoming offended and suspicious. The husbands of the victims had iron-clad alibis from the reports I read, but were treated as suspects even after they were cleared and grieving. The fact that autopsies had to be performed, burials delayed, and the victims' bodies were viewed by non-Muslims deeply angered the husbands. I think the ME's office tried to be sensitive, but the community was already upset with the initial investigators' handling of the first two cases. By the time the task force was formed, the damage was done. This is why I got sent here. I had been out of the loop since the Friday Stalker case and was on medical leave. I believed I was on vacation and probably would not have come home had I known about the killings. I walked into this blind!"

"Well," Jonah said, manipulating his mouse. "Now that we know we are looking for the same serial killer I can tell you why SID is involved in the Ten-Count case." Jonah selected the file on the computer screen labeled 10C-1.

The Killer

The killer sat low in the vehicle behind the steering wheel. A dark hooded pullover, gloves, and night vision glasses hid the killer's head, hands, and face. This was the fifth day of watching the 6 of 10 family's daily routine. The killer kept a time log of when the husband left for work and when the school-aged children were taken to the Muslim school and dropped off. This left 6 of 10 with the baby for most of the day. Tonight, the family's nighttime activities were being logged meticulously by way of the glasses and binoculars.

The street was bumper to bumper with parked cars and no one seemed to notice the killer during the previous days of watching 6 of 10. The killer changed vehicles frequently and chose older models to blend in with the cars on the street. The killer dressed as a Muslim woman during the daytime stalking.

The killer was frustrated with this deceiver, because she had company almost every day and never at the same time, or else she was driving to the store, visiting a friend, or going to some kind of meeting at the mosque. It was too dangerous trying to take her out at the Arab grocery store where she shopped. Killing 3 of 10 at the Wal-Mart had been a mistake, and the killer had barely escaped detection. It was too public a place and, really, the time to savor the kill had been too short.

Eyes closed, the image of the 6 of 10 deceiver's knee length single braid of coal black hair caused the killer's hands to tremble and pulse race. Creeping through the back yard two nights ago had been a necessary risk in order to peer into the kitchen widow. The husband and older children were at home but in another room in the house. She had been standing with her back to the window cooking, and her head was uncovered. It was all the killer could manage not to break in right then. The hair trophy dominated the killer's thoughts for two days. The deceiver's evil face must be destroyed and the braid taken. She was the last deceiver in Arizona and the killer needed to move on to where the next deceiver, 7 of 10, could be identified.

I-SID Investigation

Jonah handed Rainey the second file folder. They had just completed a review of the 10C-1 case file when Rainey's cell phone rang.

"Excuse me, Jonah," Rainey said as she saw the caller was Sara. Rainey got up from the chair and walked the distance of the room away from Jonah and angled her position so her back was slightly turned away from him.

"Hello Sara...what do you need?" Rainey asked in a neutral tone of voice.

"I just got off the phone with the boss. I typed up our reports and faxed them to him. He is absolutely livid about how you conducted yourself at the meeting with Lieutenant Jerald. He said you have his number on Voice Messaging and you haven't answered his last six calls. He really blew his top when he asked where we were, and I had to tell him I was at the house while you were out visiting some of your Muslim friends, and I couldn't tell him who the friends were or where they lived!" Sara's high pitched voice was near a screech as she paused to catch her breath. "Where in the Sam Hill are you? You've been gone for hours. Oh, and DC said to tell you that the captain is legit as far as being a captain in the US Army assigned to their Special Investigations Division. He also said that the captain is on an extended leave...

no other information was available. DC said that when you set up a meeting with him I am to be present and take the lead as the field investigator representing the FBI in all matters. DC also said to tell you that you are jeopardizing your job maybe your entire career and he expects you to call ASAP. Are you going to call him now?"

Rainey waited for Sara to wind down. After a few seconds of silence Rainey responded to Sara. "You should know better than anyone that I don't need the job at the FBI. DC's threats are empty words and he should realize that. He hasn't a leg to stand on as I am doing exactly what he and the task force requested me to do. I'm acting as a liaison with the Muslim community and gathering information."

"I told him all that," Sara said defensively.

"Also Sara, I am well over the legal age for adulthood. I'm single, independent, and on my vacation. I don't need a babysitter and I don't need your permission to visit my friends. I don't have to tell you who I am visiting or where. Is that clear enough for you?" Rainey heard what she thought was Sara gulping and holding back tears. She knew her so well and could visualize Sara's face with a hurt look and tears brimming in her eyes. It also hurt Rainey a lot to talk to her best friend as she just did.

"Rainey we can't sort this all out by phone. I can't stand you being so upset with me. We need to talk and find a way to work this out. The task force needs your help. I need your help. The Muslim community needs your help. I know you are working hard at forming trust and ties, Rainey, and I told DC that. I told him it was stupid how he and his PPD buddy had set this whole thing up. And I don't want to meet the captain by myself. Our two heads together are better than me working this alone. My instincts tell me he has some key information and it doesn't look like he wants to talk to anyone but you."

"I'll be home in about another two hours, Sara. Wait up for me and we'll talk," Rainey said in a friendlier tone.

"Okay, Rainey. I'll be waiting." Sara broke the connection.

Jonah remained silent, waiting for Rainey to speak. Rainey walked back across the room and sat down next to him again. The silence in the room lengthened. Jonah could see that Rainey was trying to come to a decision about something related to the phone call and he did not want to break her thought process.

"That was Sara…you knew that," Rainey said as an afterthought.

"Any new problems I can help with?" Jonah asked.

"Maybe yes and maybe no…you'll have to decide," Rainey replied. Jonah waited again for Rainey to continue.

"I'd like for us to review the 10C-2 file first, and then discuss a plan of action." Rainey said. Jonah nodded agreement and they got to work.

An hour later Rainey flexed the fingers of her left hand and then stood and stretched. Jonah did a few stretching exercises, too. It had been an intense hour, but they had identified some important factors that would help them catch the serial killer.

"You've done a lot of ground work, Jonah. I understand why the government has tried to walk on eggs. Identifying the one killer could create an international outcry. I know you need to be certain it is a military person who did the killings and perhaps is now ex-military continuing the killing here in Arizona."

Jonah answered, "After a year I have narrowed the list to three individuals who served in the Army Reserves. All three are no longer active duty and are stateside. The two males and one female have gone off the map. About six months ago the known addresses for the two males were checked and they had moved and not left forwarding addresses. I've contacted friends and family and got nothing. It's as if they don't exist anymore. The female went missing right after she returned stateside. No one has seen or heard from her, either. And all my leads have come to a dead end…until the killings began here in Arizona and that's what brought me here."

"You've ruled out civilian contractors who were in both countries at the times of the killings?"

"Yes. It was exhaustive, but we focused on the towns where the killings took place. The killers could have been stationed in different locations, but that is unlikely as movement in those countries is, at best, risky, and closely tracked," Jonah replied.

"There's a lot in these reports that is redacted, Jonah."

"I know, but you are seeing what I am authorized to disseminate."

Rainey sighed but didn't argue the point. "Do you have a priority for most to least likely as the serial killer for the three suspects? " Rainey asked.

"Well my boss and everyone else involved in our Ten-Count investigation think it most likely one of the two males. What do you think? You've read all five case files now."

Rainey pursed her lips and looked at the pictures of the *1 of 10* and *2 of 10* victims. The MO of the killer was identical down to the cutting of the hair and taking it as a trophy.

"I wouldn't so easily dismiss the female. The method of killing was poison in three of the killings and by knife for the other two. Poison is known to be a method of choice for female killers, and many female killers prefer knives over guns. It wouldn't have taken a lot of physical strength to overcome any of the victims in the right circumstances," Rainey spoke softly as her brows knitted together as she formed her next thoughts.

"What kind of circumstances," Jonah prompted Rainey.

"Say it is the female. She puts on an abeya, hijab…scarf, and gloves. She researches Islamic practices so she knows how to mingle within a crowd of Muslim women without any notice. Many immigrant Muslim women are shy about talking with people they don't know, even other Muslim women. It would be easy to just give the Islamic greeting and sit through any number of women's meetings with minimal verbal contact."

"A male could dress up and disguise himself if he wore the face veil, too, right?" Jonah asked.

"It's possible, but it would be harder to keep up the disguise if he was around at prayer time. He'd have to go into the ladies room and uncover partially to do the ceremonially washing called *wudu* of hands, head, face, feet, and arms. Men also walk differently," Rainey replied.

"Both the males are under 5' 6" in height, both weigh less than 150 pounds, and both are what would be considered small framed for a male. They wouldn't stand out like many males would," Jonah commented. "Got anything else that could point to our female suspect being the killer?"

"The locations of the killings and times of the killings," Rainey said.

"Explain," Jonah asked. Rainey could hear a tremor of excitement in his voice. She felt it too.

"All five killings happened in locations where women would normally be expected to be found…their homes or a women's rest room. All five killings happened during the day when most Muslim women are at home or shopping and their husbands are at work or out of the house. I was thinking about a sister showing up at the front door carrying a dish or baked goods to share and spend some time visiting or reading the Qur'an with the victim. If a man showed up, he would not be admitted under any circumstances, but another sister bearing a gift of time and a home cooked dish to share… a male killer disguised as a Muslim woman or the female suspect might be invited into the home…welcomed even."

"This would account for no forced entries in the four home slayings," Jonah stated.

"Could be that the victims didn't have their back doors locked because of children playing in the yards outside," Rainey responded.

Rainey paused and then very quickly began looking through the file folder on the female suspect. After searching a few pages she found what she was looking for. "The female suspect's maternal aunt lived in Mesa, Arizona during the years she was a teenager. It's possible that our female suspect visited her aunt frequently on vacations and holidays. It's probable that she's familiar with the Arizona locations. It says here that the aunt was killed last year in an auto accident. Did anyone talk to the neighbors about knowing the suspect?" Rainey asked.

Jonah took the report and went over each page of interview statements. "Nothing in the reports," he replied.

"Let's check on the two male suspects and see if there are any possible ties that got over-looked by the first investigator," Rainey said, as she picked up one file folder and handed Jonah the other.

"One of the male suspects attended two years of high school in Yuma, AZ. His parents divorced and his mother moved back east taking him and his two brothers with her. The background on him doesn't show anything unusual other than the divorce, if divorce can be called unusual. Nobody seems to remember him from the interviews with the school, neighbors and classmates we located. He was basically a loner—no problems on record with the law or school. The other suspect's background doesn't indicate he is known to have ever lived in Arizona or had or has family or relatives living in Arizona," Jonah recapped for Rainey.

"I like for our prime suspect the female, with the Arizona male as second and the other male third," Rainey stated.

"I'd like to read the task force case files on the Arizona victims and their profiles before I can make a decision about a primary suspect," Jonah said.

"Fair enough," Rainey replied. "It's getting late and we have a big surprise for Sara. I have all my task force files in a mini murder room Sara and I set up in one of the bedrooms of my house. You can read the files and profiles once we get there. You agree that it's time to begin working together with the task force and Sara?" Rainey asked.

Jonah agreed and began putting the files and laptop in the wall safe so they could get started for Rainey's home. Rainey put her notes in a large folder Jonah gave her that held copies of the two Ten-Count reports.

As they stood by their cars in the parking lot, Rainey said to Jonah, "I'm glad you agreed that it's time to meet with Lieutenant Jerald. If you don't want to meet with the entire task force and blow your cover, I understand. I think I can get Sara to set up a meet between the four of us. The sooner the better, as I have this terrible feeling that we are almost out of time. We need to pool our information and work together."

"Let's talk to Sara and pick her brain. We didn't discuss the killer's trophies and their possible significance to the killer and a possible motive or motives. Maybe a third and fourth set of eyes and ears can help in this area?" Jonah replied as he got ready to close the door to his car. He didn't wait for an answer. He followed Rainey's car out of the underground parking area and they turned east on McDowell Road heading back to Rainey's house in Tempe.

Rainey pulled into the carport and Jonah parked behind her. The front porch light went out and Rainey saw the living room window curtain move slightly. That was Sara checking to see who had come home with Rainey. The front porch light came back on, and Sara was standing in the open doorway. Rainey could see she was angry. It was almost midnight and she had told Sara she would be home at least an hour ago.

"What in the hell is he doing here?" Sara's raised voice demanded.

Rainey brushed past Sara who barely moved out of the doorway for Jonah to follow Rainey into the house. The front door slammed shut and Sara stood with her back against it. Sara stared hard at Rainey and ignored Jonah.

"We could use some coffee, Sara. We have a lot of ground to cover tonight… ah...this morning and once we share what we've been doing with you, I want you to call Lieutenant Jerald and have him come to the house at, say, 2 AM. We haven't got much time, Sara. No time for petty arguments and recriminations. We have a lot of work to do if we are going to get this killer before there is another body. Let's call a truce and put personal and Bureau stuff aside for now. Agreed?"

Sara looked steadily at Rainey and then Jonah. Slowly she nodded her head and moved from the front door. Jonah breathed a sigh of relief. He hadn't sat down, but had been watching the two friends and waiting to take his cue from Rainey.

Rainey walked into the dining room and put the files Jonah gave her on the table. Sara was pouring the coffee into three cups and saw Rainey give the captain a key to the mini murder room. "The captain… Jonah… is going to go back and read the files and the work we have in the back room, and you are going to sit and read the case files on 1 of 10 and 2 of 10 from SID and Interpol. The three of us are then going to talk and then you are going to call Lieutenant Jerald and tell him it is imperative he come here ASAP. Okay?"

Sara looked surprised then she nodded agreement. She handed Jonah a cup of coffee from the tray and set the tray down on the table. She sat down and slid the file over, picked out the 10C-1 file, and opened it. Jonah took his cue from Sara, and without a word, headed down the hallway to the padlocked door. He went inside and closed the door.

Rainey walked into the living room and curled up in Grams' recliner. Her shoulder ached as did her head. Rainey closed her eyes and decided to take a short cat nap. Within seconds she had fallen into a restless sleep.

✳ ✳ ✳

"Rainey, wake up," Sara's gentle voice and touch slowly aroused Rainey as she opened her protesting eyes and moved her stiff muscles.

Rainey looked at Sara and Jonah sitting on the couch watching her. "What? Have I missed something?" Rainey spoke to both of them. She didn't like the look on their faces. "Did you call Lieutenant Jerald? Where is he? How long have I been asleep?" Rainey asked.

"The lieutenant should be here in about twenty minutes. He was delayed because I caught him at a homicide scene and you've been asleep two hours." Sara told Rainey.

"Homicide scene? Not 6 of 10?" Rainey said feeling dread spread throughout her body. *They were too late. Too late!* Her mind screamed at her.

"It wasn't 6 of 10, Rainey. It was one of their own. A city officer assigned to headquarters. He worked the front desk," Sarah said.

"But why would the task force commander be working a homicide? Unless…does it have something to do with the SKTF cases?"

"When he called, he didn't give many details. He said he'd explain when he got here," Jonah answered Rainey.

"He knows about you?" Rainey asked Jonah.

"I gave him a very sketchy briefing, and he sounded relieved not ticked off, thankfully."

"That's some progress. Now we just wait," Rainey said, unable to suppress a yawn.

Investigations Merge

Rainey saw the headlamps shining on the front window and heard the car motor stop. A door slammed and Rainey opened the front door as Lieutenant Jerald walked sluggishly towards her. His shoulders were slumped, head bent down, and his clothes wrinkled and disheveled. As he lifted his head to address her, she saw heavy pouches below his eyes and deep lines creasing the sides of his face. He looked like he had aged ten years in 48 hours. It was hard losing a brother officer... hard. It reminded every officer how fleeting life could be.

"Morning Lieutenant," Rainey greeted him somberly.

Lieutenant Jerald nodded and said, "Rainey" as he came through the doorway and headed for Grams recliner and sat down heavily.

"Can we get you some coffee or water? Something to eat" Sara asked him.

"Coffee, black," he said and smiled his gratitude at Sara. He looked over at the couch where Jonah was sitting. "You must be Captain Daniels, US Army, SID?"

"Call me Jonah." Jonah stood and walked over to the lieutenant with his arm extended. The two men shook hands briefly.

"Everyone calls me Robert," the lieutenant said, as he sat back down. He looked like he might have fallen down if the chair was not behind him.

Rainey, Sara, and Jonah waited while the lieutenant sipped his coffee. He'd talk when he was ready.

As Jerald put his cup down he looked at Rainey and Sara. "Remember the desk officer at headquarters? You both met him this week. Everyone calls...called...him Willie...Sergeant Timothy Williams. He was found murdered and butchered in his apartment around midnight by a neighbor getting off the late shift from work...another Phoenix PD officer. His door was left wide open, and he was laying a few feet from the doorway. His body was staged. The killer wanted him found...made it easy." The lieutenant paused and brushed his hand across his eyes.

Rainey had seen the moisture there, but said nothing, just listened, as did Sara and Jonah.

"That arrogant psycho cut out his tongue, put it between his hands folded across Willie's belly, and stuck one of those damn yellow Post-it notes on his forehead. The text was block-printed and said...*collateral damage!* That's why I was called to the scene."

"But the sergeant is a man and he's not a Muslim. He's not even on the task force," Sara said, not comprehending how the desk sergeant, a non field officer, could be connected to the serial killer.

"The psycho also put a zero below the text. Wanted us to know how much contempt he had for Willie or maybe for the Phoenix PD. I just don't know at this point. There was no sign of a struggle. Very little evidence except the Post-it note. Not even any stray fibers or hair to collect that we know of at this point. The murder weapon was not left at the scene, either."

"I can't believe Sergeant Williams just stood there and let some maniac cut out his tongue and slit his throat without putting up a good fight," Sara said.

"The Sergeant was not a small man. Sure he had a wide girth around the middle, but he would have fought for his life," Rainey said. She felt certain of that.

"It had to be someone he knew and trusted. He didn't see it coming," the lieutenant replied. "The ME called to the scene told me that the killer got close enough to Willie to sever his spinal cord and paralyze him. He said it looked to him like something he had seen done in combat-military situations."

"Jesus…while Willie was still breathing the psycho put him on his back, cut out his tongue and put it in Willie's hands. Then the killer plunged a knife repeatedly into Willie's stomach a dozen times before finishing him off by stabbing him in the heart." Lieutenant Jerald shuddered. Sara and Rainey's faces turned pale and they looked at the lieutenant somberly.

"The neighbor who found him…the other officer who returned home from his regular shift…you think he's clear of any involvement?" Jonah asked. Rainey noticed that Jonah seemed outwardly unaffected by Lieutenant Jerald's description of Officer Williams' slaying.

"He's our one lead. There's gonna be hell to pay in the press tomorrow if the lead goes nowhere," Lieutenant Jerald said while shaking his head. "The chief gave the okay, but I'm glad I'm a working stiff and not a political animal. Major Billings is sweating it. Shit goes downhill and it'll fall on his shoulders."

"Back up a minute," Jonah said. "Why would the Phoenix PD and your task force be rousting the press-media? How do they figure into all this?"

"The officer who found him told us Willie had been bragging about working with some muckity-muck investigative reporter working the Scarf Killer slayings. Willie couldn't resist telling him that he and this reporter were going to break the case. The reporter would get a national byline and a book contract for the story, and Willie was going to get a detective shield. I've got half the PD force hauling in reporters and conducting interviews. They are screaming foul and threatening to sue. It's a real mess."

Rainey and Sara sat there with their mouths almost hanging open. This case just kept getting more complicated. And the worst part of it was they didn't have one single clue as to what was motivating this killer. Why he selected who to kill…and, Rainey kept this thought to herself, she wasn't convinced they were looking for a male.

For the next hour, Jonah and Robert sat in the dining room and briefed each other on the SK/Ten-Count cases and discussed possible leads from the latest victim, Sergeant Williams. While they talked, Sara and Rainey sat in the living room and worked out the issues that had built up between them…all related to how their boss had handled their assignments.

Jonah and the lieutenant agreed they had one killer, but disagreed on whether the killer was male or female. They planned to meet with Major Billings at Phoenix PD later in the morning. Lieutenant Jerald would give them a call from headquarters after he got there. Sara and Rainey were invited to the meeting, but Rainey had her own meetings scheduled with the Muslim leaders. Sara accepted though, and Jonah offered to give her a ride to headquarters later after they got the call from Lieutenant Jerald. Jonah agreed to bunk down on Rainey's couch for a few hours of sleep.

Lieutenant Jerald shook Jonah's hand and prepared to leave. He'd already received six calls and was urgently needed back a headquarters.

The Killer

The killer sat on the couch fondling the trophies. Calm now, energy spent, and suffused with a feeling of relaxation the killer gloated at the night's work. Loose ends were taken care of now. That stupid imbecile and his big mouth…he could have spoiled everything. Willie was a warning that the killer had been careless because of curiosity. Wanting to know who those two women were could have been the killer's undoing. But that small problem was taken care of. Blubber gut wouldn't be bragging any more.

A small nagging worry intruded on the victory celebration. *Who had that pig talked to?*

The killer stood and began to pace. Forming a relationship with the pig had been a sloppy move…a mistake. Mistakes could ruin the mission and cost freedom or life. No more mistakes.

Tomorrow, the house would be leased, clothing and personal items shipped, and the utilities opened by the lease manager. A new car would be rented and left parked in the storage shed. *I'll torch this house tomorrow and stay overnight in the storage shed. The next day 6 of 10 will cease to exist and by late afternoon I'll be on my way.*

A high pitched laugh came from the killer's mouth. It would take the task force at least two weeks to figure out that the Scarf Killer was gone.

Two more days, and then on the hunt again. Four names left on the list. They didn't deserve to live, but death and justice would be at their door soon. Then peace...the obligation completed... duty done. It would then be time to go home.

Checkmate

Sara closed the door behind Lieutenant Jerald and massaged her temples. "I've got a whopper of a headache. Any Tylenol in the medicine cabinet, Rainey?"

"Not in the guest bathroom, but in the bathroom off of my bedroom," Rainey said as she plunked down a pillow, sheet, and blanket on the couch next to Jonah.

"I'm going to call the boss and let him know what's been happening. He can wait on a written report sometime later today after the meeting with the task force. We have a few hours before we have to be at Phoenix PD and I'm gonna spend that time sleeping," Sara declared. She gave Rainey a quick hug, nodded at Jonah, and walked down the hallway.

"Jonah, I know you are tired. I'm beat, too, but what we haven't talked about much is the possible motives and how or why the killer selects each victim. Did Lieutenant Jerald have any ideas?"

"We both agreed that by combining the two investigations we can sift through everything fairly quickly and send the data to the FBI Profiler Division. He's going to meet with Major Billings and ask him to call your boss to get clearance. He'll be sending the evidence reports by courier and faxing everything else. We might even hear something later on today if your boss gets started on this right away. But as long as Jerald is stubbornly convinced the killer is male and also a local news reporter, it will be hard to persuade him the killer is female. ”

"So why didn't you speak more forcefully about the reasons we think the killer is female?"

Jonah didn't respond.

"I still don't know what in your investigation caused you to start tracking down current and former service men and women. The reports you showed me had so much information redacted and you know what is left out of those reports. You haven't told me how you came up with the list of Muslim names you want me to check with the imams. You didn't bring this up with Robert, did you? I bet you didn't mention anything to Sara either," Rainey said. The accusation was stark and Jonah looked like she'd slapped him in the face. "You're still holding back."

"The military and civilian leaders in our government want to avoid the embarrassment and an international outcry. I already told you that. They believe the morale of the troops in combat areas will be negatively impacted if this investigation gets out into the civilian press. The bureaucrats felt that SID and Interpol could track down the killer and keep the entire murder and investigation within the military and out of the civilian media. As long as the killer stayed out of the USA, that was possible. Even after I reported that the three deaths in Arizona were likely to be linked to the first two deaths, my superiors insisted I get a confirmation…"

Rainey interrupted, "The yellow Post-it notes is the information you needed to confirm, right?"

"Right. And once confirmed, I was authorized to use my judgment on how much information to share with local law enforcement. Until tonight when the killer went off the chart and killed Officer Williams, I still thought I could, with your help, find the killer and stay out of the SKTF investigation," Jonah said, and shook his head as if he wanted to reject what he knew he had to do.

"So what connects your list of suspects to the list of Muslim names is the killer's motive. You have known this from the onset, Jonah."

"Rainey, all I can offer is the fact that I am following orders," Jonah responded.

"So if Sergeant Williams hadn't been killed and the media dragged into the investigation by the task force…you would not have agreed to meet with the task force commander later this morning. You used my anger at Sara, my boss, and the task force to get the information you needed…now what…you go after the killer? Take out the killer and then disappear into the sunset?" Rainey demanded speaking each word harshly…her breath ragged…her face tight with anger.

Jonah's body became tense and his voice remote when he answered, "You are correct."

"If you want my help getting a complete list of names from the Muslim community then you better come clean, Jonah, else any information you get from me will come from the SKTF. Showing up at the task force meeting later this morning and sending information to the FBI profiler…it's all a stalling tactic, isn't it? I don't know what you told Sara, I was asleep. I don't know what you told Lieutenant Jerald…you withheld information from both of them, didn't you? If you'd told Lieutenant Jerald everything he wouldn't still be convinced the killer is a male and thinking he's looking for a killer who is a male news reporter!" Rainey's disbelief and anger were mounting as Jonah sat there staring straight ahead without showing an ounce of emotion. The man was stone cold.

"I want the list of names the killer is using to target her victims, Jonah, and I want to know why you believe this female is killing Muslim women!"

Phoenix Headquarters – SKTF

Lieutenant Jerald parked in the back employee's lot. He turned off the ignition and sat back in his seat, closing his eyes for a few moments. *Jesus…poor Willie*, he thought. He glanced at his wrist watch, 7 AM. It was going to be a very long day. He could hear the angry voices of the press crowding the steps to the entrance of the police department. More reporters milled together on the sidewalk, trying to block the employee entrance to the back parking lot. Officers cleared a path so he could get through. He didn't envy them having to deal with the mob.

Captain Jonathan Daniels, SID-Interpol…he wasn't playing straight. There was something he was holding back. The lieutenant continued to sit in his unmarked vehicle thinking about it. *Agent Walker…I was wrong about her. She's okay, but her buddy, Sara James…she was like the SID captain…hell…Billing's buddy DC Britt, too, had his own agenda. I don't trust any of them.*

Pieces are missing from the Ten-Count investigations. His instincts told him this, but he was too tired and overwhelmed to sort it out now. He didn't trust the task force partners farther than he could keep them in sight. Inter-agency politics was bad enough, but when multiple agencies with their own agendas started throwing their weight around, it wasn't good for any investigation. He had a sinking feeling that if they didn't start working together soon there would be another victim.

He couldn't delay any longer. Major Billings was waiting for him. He walked to the back entrance and took the elevator up to the second floor. As the elevator opened, his ears were assaulted by the clamor and strident voices of reporters and officers spilling out from the conference room into the hallway. He was right… attempting to interview the hundreds of reporters led to shouting matches and protests. The reporters, predictably, claimed a right to protect their sources and provided little more than their contact information.

The voices of the reporters in the hallway momentarily ceased when they saw Lieutenant Jerald step out of the elevator. They rushed toward him, yelling his name, demanding to know information, threatening to sue him, the City, and the police department. He pushed his way through the crowd of angry reporters, down the hallway, to the task force conference room. He hit the buzzer and someone inside opened the locked door for him. He quickly went through the door and when it closed he heard the lock click in place.

"Hiding out, Major?" Lieutenant Jerald asked, seeing the major drumming his fingers on the conference table.

"It's about time. I've been here for two hours waiting on you. You better have something to tell me that I can give to that pack of wolves outside, Lieutenant! The chief will be holding a press conference at eight o'clock and he doesn't want to look like a fool. How in the hell did one of our desk sergeants become involved in this investigation and end up a victim? What does the "0" and "collateral damage" message have to do with it? Hauling in every reporter in the city has just made matters worse, Jerald!"

Lieutenant Jerald knew better than to remind the major that he had given the order to haul in the press and interview them at headquarters. The chief and Billings were now dealing with the mayor and council, who were worried about, among other things, lawsuits. The lieutenant knew the major cared about every last one of the officers under his command even if sometimes he didn't show it...like now.

"Major Billings, as far as we know at this point, Sergeant Williams was acting on his own and outside departmental regulations."

Major Billings sighed. "That can lessen the negativity for the Department overall, but it may come down hard on the uniform division commander and Sergeant William's immediate supervisor. Have notifications to the family been made yet?"

Lieutenant Jerald took a small spiral notebook from his jacket pocket and flipped through a few pages. "Captain Michaels and Lieutenant Rodriguez, Uniform Division, did the notification in person at his sister's home. The parents are deceased. An officer from the Line-of-Duty Death unit and a Catholic Chaplain from the Family Support Group organization arrived and stayed with the sister and her family. They will help the family through what needs to be done and provide departmental ongoing support."

"Line of duty death ribbons and bands are being distributed to all department personnel. Counselors are on notice to be available, especially for friends and co-workers of Sergeant Williams. I'll advise you when the wake and funeral arrangements are solid. Patrol Bureau will be handling all department notifications and keep the chief informed as well."

"How did the sergeant get involved in your investigation?"

"A neighbor in Sergeant Williams' apartment complex is also a uniformed officer. He and the Sergeant were friends, though they worked different shifts in different squads and duty assignments." Lieutenant Jerald flipped a couple of more pages in the notebook and looked over his notes before proceeding.

"According to Officer C. 'Clemens' Ashcraft, Sergeant Williams told him on two separate occasions that he was working undercover with a big shot national investigative reporter on the SK investigation. It seems he bragged about the insider information he was getting from the reporter..."

Major Billings interrupted the lieutenant, "No doubt the Sergeant was giving more information than he was getting! You are sure the Sergeant didn't have access to the SKTF room? Have you checked to see if he hung out with any task force members or if any of them talked out of turn outside the TF?"

"Sergeant Williams didn't have access to the conference room or murder room, and I've checked with all task force members, who have all said they'd take a polygraph to prove they hadn't spoken to him or anyone else about the investigation," Lieutenant Jerald said, barely able to contain a civil tone. He knew the major would ask these questions. It just irked him that the integrity of his task force team would be questioned because of that psycho and the sergeant trying to make detective before his retirement in less than two years.

"What did you do with the officer who found Sergeant Williams? You've isolated him, right? Maybe we can keep this part of the investigation under wraps for now...at least until the killer is identified and captured."

"Major Billings, I'm doing my best at damage control. The Patrol Division commander is doing everything he can also. Every officer responding to Sergeant Williams' murder scene has been told that they talk to no one except me or the Patrol Division commander. We've done what we can, sir, to put a lid on this, but cops talk...you know that."

"If any of them talk out-of-turn and I find out, their ass will be fired," fumed the major.

"Understood."

"What else, Lieutenant?"

"Dealing with the press, sir, the legitimate press," replied Lieutenant Jerald.

"Legitimate?"

"The only way we can look at this is that the serial killer posed as an undercover investigative reporter and duped Sergeant

Williams into believing that they could both benefit if they worked together. Sergeant Williams was the killer's insider. Last night Sergeant Williams became expendable. We don't know if the sergeant figured it out, or if the killer decided he didn't need him anymore."

"What do you think, Lieutenant?" Major Billing's face showed no emotion as he concentrated on what the Lieutenant would say next.

"I think the killer has plans to take out his next victim very soon and then leave the area…maybe even leave the State. Sergeant Williams was a loose end. That SOB was so arrogant he just couldn't resist leaving his calling card—the Post-it message. He wanted to be sure we knew he slaughtered him. That psycho is laughing at all of us…thinks he's smarter than we are. I'll tell you why I think the killer may be planning to move to a new killing location in a minute, Major. First, I think we need to do something about the press…the sooner the better."

"I'm listening, Lieutenant."

"I suggest you have an immediate press conference in the auditorium. Once all the reporters are inside and seated, you explain to them that the police department got some bad intel stating a local reporter was involved in the killing late last night of Sergeant Tim Williams. This led to the round up and began the process of police interviewing the local press. You tell them that in the last thirty minutes, the Department has verified that the intel was false, so all interviews are immediately discontinued. Interview reports will not placed in police records. You then thank the press for their patience and understanding. With that you lead into a short description about Sergeant Williams' career with the Phoenix PD and tell the press his killing has saddened the entire force, chief, mayor, and City Council. You tell them an intensive investigation is underway.

"And questions about the SK task force investigation?" Major Billings asked.

"If they ask you about the serial killing investigation/task force you tell them you will not be answering questions now, but there will be a major news briefing at 2 PM with the chief. You'll have time to brief the chief before then. She can say a few words and then turn it over to you and you can respond to press questions or you can turn it over to me…whatever you and the chief think best. This gives us time to get some prepared statements ready for the press."

"Robert, I think this might work. I have time to talk with the brass and we can get prepared for a major news conference this afternoon. Separating the press round up from a major update of the SK investigation may help separate the two in the minds of the press…at least temporarily, until things cool down. Good thinking, Lieutenant!"

"It just may tick off the killer and make him careless. He wanted everyone to know about how he duped the Phoenix PD… thumbing his nose at us. He'll be disappointed when he gets no press time on Willie's murder," Lieutenant Jerald replied.

"Maybe flush the killer into the open?"

"It could work out that way," replied the lieutenant.

"Now I need to know what is going on with Agent Walker, if she's made any progress with the Muslim community. The agent from the FBI staying with Walker—Agent James, doesn't seem to have a whole lot to offer the task force so far, except the information about an Army captain from SID nosing around and trying to hook up with Agent Walker."

"Sir, if we can take care of the immediate press problem now… I'll need another hour of your time, in your office, to update you on Daniels *and* Agent Walker. My team needs to get back in here and get to work."

"Let's get moving then, Lieutenant." The major stood and walked to the door, squared his shoulders and got ready to meet an angry press.

Motive

Rainey stood with her arms at her sides and hands clenched into tight fists. She was mad enough at Jonah to slug him. "I'm not asking again, Captain Daniels. There are six people dead now. I need to know why the lists of Muslim names in the communities are so important to you. Either you are looking for a killer among the Muslims or you are looking for the killer's next victims. Which is it, Captain?"

Jonah brought his hard gaze back to Rainey. He looked at her steadily without blinking for what seemed like minutes to Rainey, but was only a few seconds. Jonah made a decision he hoped he would not regret.

"I'd like to give you a list of specific questions I need to know about some members who will be listed by the Muslim leaders. The questions will be a sort of process of elimination and whittle down the number of names…at least it should do that. In other words, I only need the names of Muslims living in these communities who meet these very specific criteria. Will you do this for me, for the safety and lives of these people, Rainey?"

"They're the victims aren't they, Captain? You showed me the three suspect files, but no photos, no names. All identifying information was blacked out. I know you think it's the female suspect…I know it, Captain. I don't understand why you didn't press this point home with the lieutenant, but I have my suspicions. I'll share the information I get with you and with the task force, but I want to know the motive. You darn well know it, and it is important. Your orders or not, the task force has a right to know."

Jonah knew that Rainey could not be sweet-talked, and also knew that if they didn't find the suspect soon, she would disappear, taking more police lives and as well as the original intended victims. As far as he was concerned, Rainey and the rest of them were losing their usefulness and were incapable of seeing the big picture. "My job is to track down this serial killer and return the killer to the custody of the US Army. The Army *is* the authority over this killer. Putting the killer behind bars until a military trial is held will close the SK serial killer investigation, and there will be no 6 of 10. This is a military matter, Agent Walker."

"You aren't much different, are you Captain Daniels, from the first SID officer? No…you're worse. At least the other officer was an *honest* ass!" Rainey's voice shook with her anger and contempt.

Jonah shrugged his shoulders. His voice showed no emotion when he asked, "Will you ask the questions on the list?"

Rainey felt sick inside…but she knew she had no choice. If she agreed to ask the questions, he'd give her the list, and if she asked the questions, then she'd have names to provide the task force.

"Yes. I'll ask the imams to tell me which Muslims on their membership lists fit your criteria," she replied.

"Good."

Rainey watched as the captain reached down and picked up a briefcase leaning against the side of the couch. He hadn't brought the briefcase in with him when they arrived. *He must have had it in his trunk,* Rainey thought.

As Jonah opened the briefcase and took out a sheet of paper, he commented, "I brought it inside while you were taking your nap."

Rainey wondered what else he had done while she was asleep. He was supposed to have briefed Sara. Rainey took the paper from the captain's outstretched hand and quickly scanned the typed questions.

"The motive for the killings, Captain Daniels. You agreed to give me that."

"When you bring me the names later today, you have my word as a sworn law enforcement officer I will give you that information then."

Rainey was about to protest, but stopped when she saw him raise his hand.

"Your last meeting is at three. I'll meet you at Rosita's at four. Don't be late Rainey, and don't drag Sara or the task force along. You can meet with them afterwards."

Jonah stood up, picked up his briefcase, and walked towards the front door. "Please apologize to Sara for me. I won't be able to give her a ride to Phoenix headquarters later. I will call Lieutenant Jerald and make my apologies for missing the briefing later today."

Rainey just sat where she was and watched as he opened the door and then closed it quietly behind him. *Sara is going to be blown away when I tell her about this,* Rainey thought as she got up and walked to the dining room. There was no point in trying to take a nap. Rainey was in such turmoil, she knew sleep would evade her. She'd type up the notes she had taken earlier in the captain's office and do the report for DC. It would save Sara a lot of work and she owed her.

Double Cross

Rainey looked at the table for her papers from Jonah's office. Her hand written notes and the file folder with copies of the case files were not on the table. "Sara must have taken them to the murder room," Rainey thought out loud, as she turned and walked down the hallway. The door to the murder room was not locked. *Sara knows better*, Rainey thought as she turned the handle and opened the door.

Ten minutes later Rainey had thoroughly searched the room. The information Jonah had given her was nowhere to be found. Rainey was starting to panic. She told herself to slow down. "The file and notes are probably in Sara's room," Rainey spoke out loud as she closed the murder room door, locked it, and hurried to Sara's bedroom.

Sara was out cold. She didn't hear Rainey come into the room and quietly search. She woke with a start and reached for her Smith & Wesson and then realized it was Rainey yelling her name. "Sara! Sara! Wake up!"

"What's happened, Rainey? Are you okay? What's wrong?" Sara looked at the alarm clock. It wasn't quite seven o'clock. Sara didn't feel much better for the two hours of sleep.

"Sara where is the file folder of the Ten-Count investigation and the notes I brought with me when I came home…the intel the captain gave me?"

"I left them on the work table in the Murder room. Why?"

"The file and notes are gone. I searched everywhere."

"What? How can they just disappear?"

"Did you see him go outside to his car and bring in a briefcase and take it back to the murder room?"

"Yes." Sara started to share Rainey's dread. "Where's Jonah?

"He's gone, Sara. Did you make him copies of the SKTF files?"

"He asked me for copies and as he'd given us copies of the Ten-Count case files and it's all the same case now…well, I didn't think you would care. Did he skip on us?"

"We've been double crossed. He oh so politely told me to please tell you he would not be able to give you a ride to the task force meeting this morning, and he wouldn't be at the meeting. He has copies of the task force case files, your notes, my notes, insider information from Lieutenant Jerald and what do we have? We have zilch…nada…and a captain gone AWOL."

Rainey sank down onto the edge of the bed and bent over placing her head in her hands. "I just want to scream, Sara."

Sara had got up from the bed and was now pacing back and forth in front of Rainey. "What can he be up to?"

"I don't know, Sara, honestly. He gave me a list of very specific questions to ask the imams today about the Muslims on their community member listings. He told me he only needed the names of the Muslims fitting this exact criteria. I asked if these people were the potential SK victims. He didn't say no, but he didn't say yes, either. I pressed him hard about what he knew about the killer's motive. He knows, Sara. I'm sure of it."

"What did he say, Rainey?"

"He said when I meet him later this afternoon with the information from the Muslim leaders, he'll tell me."

"Do you believe him?"

"Oh, he swore as an officer of the US Army and as a law enforcement officer, but…no…I don't trust him…he's too smooth. He lies too much, and he's good at it."

Sara looked thoughtful. "You know, all is not lost. By giving you the list of questions to match to the list of names, I bet with Zarinah's help, we can identify 6 of 10."

Rainey looked at her friend. "Yes, and we'll have a good idea of how to find the next victims, too. We can find these people and protect them…maybe set a trap for the killer."

"Rainey, if you are worried about what Robert or DC is gonna say—remember the lieutenant sat in your dining room trading intel with the captain for over an hour. Jonah is about the best I've ever come across when it comes to running an operation. He's been light years ahead of us all the way!"

"Sara I've got a feeling time has almost run out. I think the captain thinks so, too. There's only one more target in this area, and then she will be moving on to the next location. Killing Sergeant Williams was cleanup in preparation of moving out. The killer knows where her victims are and may already have set things in motion to begin stalking them. Once she strikes 6 of 10, she'll be gone."

"Rainey you keep saying 'she.' Are you certain we are after a female?"

"My own reasoning is that a female could easily gain access to the Muslim women by visiting them in their homes. All the killer would need to do is wear Muslim women's outer clothing and carry the weapon and a dish of food. A Muslim woman receiving a guest with food would naturally serve it right away to show her appreciation to her guest. Four out of five killings were done by poison. The female suspect is a nurse so she very well might have medical knowledge about poisons. A women's restroom in a Wal-Mart seems like too much risk for a male…unless he was in disguise as a Muslim female. But what clinched it for me was, in my opinion, the killer's biggest mistake. *That* was killing Sergeant Williams, who was more likely to have been fooled by a female masquerading as a reporter, because she could have flattered his ego and played up to him."

Sara murmured her agreement. "And Daniels?"

"He's been chasing this killer for almost two years. He thinks the killer is a female, and he has a lot more intel than we do. He's determined to end the killings...whatever it takes. He told me flat out that this is a military matter...the killer is under the Army's authority and it's his job to clean things up."

Rainey jumped up from the bed and said, "Hurry, Sara. Get changed. We have someplace to go and we don't have a moment to lose. I've got time before my meetings and where we're going is within walking distance of the Phoenix PD."

Rainey's mind was in overdrive. There was a chance they might catch up to Daniels before he cleared out his temporary office. It was worth a try. Sara could tail him if his car was still there, and see what he was up to before he met with Rainey again. Rainey told Sara about the office the captain had across from Phoenix PD and how the door was booby-trapped if the wrong person tried to break in. Rainey didn't like the idea, even if it was her own, of Sara working solo and tailing him...but she knew Sara was a professional and one of the best working undercover.

Rainey pulled into a parking place on a side street around the corner from the captain's temporary office. She made sure it wasn't where Daniels would be able to see the car or their approach to the underground parking lot.

"Do you think he came to his office, Rainey? I didn't spot a tail anywhere on the drive here," Sara said.

"With the captain, all bets are off. If we don't see his car, we can still check to see if the special locking mechanism is attached to the office door. If it's gone, the captain has gone to ground. I'll probably only have the one chance to see him again and that will be at our meeting later."

"What do I tell Robert if I don't end up tailing the captain all day?"

"I think you should tell him everything we know. Be sure to tell him that if he sets up surveillance on me when I go to meet the captain, he'll be a no show."

"But Jonah," Sara saw Rainey's face and rephrased, "I mean, the captain, seems willing to do almost anything underhanded to reach his objective and that's to get those names from you. You've been his target from the very beginning," Sara said.

Sara and Rainey approached the underground parking lot with some caution. They checked all three levels and the captain's car was not there.

"He could have rented another car," Sara said to Rainey as she pushed the elevator UP button.

"I don't think so, Sara. If he did...well, we'd have no idea what to look for." The elevator stopped and as they stepped out Rainey looked down the hallway and said, "We're too late!"

A cleaning woman was pushing her cart into the open doorway of what had been Daniels' office.

Sara shrugged her shoulders and then put a hand on Rainey's good arm. "We made a good try, Rainey. If he wants that information he'll show up. I'm going to walk across the street and talk to Robert. Before I do that I'm calling our boss. You have a good day, Rainey. Be careful as the killer is out there and could be watching you if she's watching the mosques for her victim. Right now she could be any female we meet that we don't know...so watch your back, you hear?"

"I'm planning on doing just that. I don't want to go from meeting to meeting today. I'm going to contact Zarinah and ask her to persuade all the imams to meet with me in a couple of hours. But before I do any of that I need to go home and get cleaned up."

Rainey and Sara parted company as they left the office building. Sara walked across the street to the Phoenix PD. Rainey walked around the corner, got in her car, and took her phone out of her purse. She dialed Zarinah and waited.

The Boss

"As salaam'alaykum, Zarinah."

"Wa 'alaykum as salaam, Rainey."

"Zarinah, I need a really important favor from you. The investigation of the murders is reaching a critical stage. I think the killer will strike again very soon, and we have to identify the next victim to protect her."

Zarinah's voice lost its jolly tone and became somber. "Rainey, just ask me. I'll do whatever I am able."

"I need for you to keep confidential what I am going to tell you. Tell no one. Can you do that?"

"Yes," Zarinah replied.

"Late last night a Phoenix police officer was killed in his home. We know the killer of the three Muslim women killed him. There was evidence left at the scene for the police to find so they would know SK did the killing. I can't explain the connection right now, Zarinah, but there is a connection. We think the killer is getting ready to leave the area, but not before trying to kill one more Muslim woman from one of the communities. I can't go into details right now, but I have a short list of questions for the imams to use against the lists of Muslim names they have put together for me. The questions may help us identify the next Muslimah. If we can identify her first, we can protect her. We might be able to use this information to trap the killer."

Rainey waited as Zarinah spoke several sentences in Arabic. She knew Zarinah was talking to God—Allah.

"I will call each of them and insist they must meet with you today. What time and where should I tell them the meeting is located?"

"Is there a place where we can have some privacy and the room large enough for all of us? Would the Phoenix mosque work?"

Zarinah thought about this for a minute. "Rainey, I think the Tempe masjid would be a better location. It's centrally located, and there is a large conference room that can be closed off. The imam can have a couple of the brothers stand outside each door to make sure no one wanders into the room. The brothers can be trusted. Both provide armed security services when threats have been made."

Rainey was momentarily at a loss for words. She hadn't realized the misunderstandings and even hate against Muslims had reached a level where armed guards would be needed for protection. It dawned upon Rainey that the armed guards at the event the other day were not just because of the serial killer. So many things had changed since she was a child and young teen growing up within these communities. September 11 and the violence that has followed for years now have affected everyone. Rainey felt a deep sadness.

"Rainey? Rainey? Are you still there?" Zarinah asked, because Rainey had not responded for some time. Zarinah thought the phone had become disconnected or Rainey's cell battery went dead.

"I'm here, Zarinah. Sorry about that. I got lost in my thoughts momentarily. The Tempe mosque will be fine. Is eleven o'clock okay for you? Will it give the imams enough time? I know you don't drive. Do you want me to pick you up?"

Rainey silently chided herself. Asking so many questions and not giving time for an answer…she'd been spending too much time with Sara!

"I think if I tell the imams we need to meet before the noon prayer at the Tempe mosque this will work best. It'll give each imam enough time to drive there and the Tempe imam time to get the room ready for us. BiBi is retired and drives me around. He's my number one chauffer. The van is fitted up for my wheelchair and it's very easy for me to get in and out."

"You are a real peach, Zarinah. Remember that it is critical that each imam bring the list of names. If a family is not included or a single Muslimah left off the lists…" Rainey didn't go on.

"I understand, Rainey, and I'll make sure the imams understand, too."

"I'll meet you at the masjid in plenty of time before the noon prayer. Thank you so much, Zarinah." Rainey put her phone back in her purse and headed for home.

Rainey signed the report and turned on the fax machine. After sending the report, she went to the kitchen to fix a sandwich and a cup of coffee. Rainey expected DC to be calling within the next ten minutes and he wasn't going to be a happy camper. Sara had heard him rant and rave the last time. It was only fair that Rainey took her turn in the barrel. She was largely responsible anyway, for breaking protocol and the SOP. Sara was more a team player and rule-follower.

The phone rang just as Rainey was putting her empty plate and cup in the kitchen sink. "Hello, DC."

"Agent Walker, you seem to have remembered what the ringing of your phone means…that's progress," DC Brit greeted Rainey with his famous sarcasm.

"I am sorry, boss. Things have really been hectic here. Sara has reported in when I couldn't and you have received daily reports, right?"

"You sound troubled, Rainey."

"I am. Sara is meeting with the task force this morning, and we're working together as a team now…but the Phoenix police officer's murder has ratcheted the stakes even higher. The killer is tying up loose ends and preparing to leave the area. If we don't identify the killer soon, 6 of 10 will die, and there's no telling where the killer will turn up until 7 of 10 is found."

"Is the task force any closer?"

"Boss, there are absolutely no clues or evidence at the crime scenes to work with…all leads have been run to the ground except…"

"Tell me what you are thinking, Rainey," DC encouraged, as Rainey hesitated before continuing with her thought.

"The task force is convinced that our killer is male and I think SK is a female. That cowboy, the Army SID officer, thinks the killer is female, and Sara is leaning in that direction."

"You called the captain a cowboy. Want to explain what you mean? I didn't see any reference to him as cowboy in any of your reports."

"Boss, something about him bothers me. He avoided contact with the task force with a plausible reason, but he did his best to isolate me from the task force and Sara by playing on my emotions. He shared a lot of intel with me…even gave me copies of the Ten-Count case files and let me take notes, et cetera. He met with Lieutenant Jerald at my house in the early morning hours. Seemed most cooperative, and when the lieutenant left my house, it was with the understanding that the captain would be at the task force meeting this morning."

"I read this in your report. Nothing looks suspicious with this," DC remarked.

"Well, he stole back all the information he gave me, plus my notes about his Ten-Count investigation, told me he would not be at the task force meeting, and well… I hate to say this but I feel like he's blackmailing me."

"You want to explain that?" DC said. A hard sound developed in DC's voice.

"He never told me why he thinks the killer is female and I am almost sure he knows who the killer is. He showed me three suspects he was tracking down and only one is female. He won't tell me why he suspects her. She's either military AWOL or prior military. He wants me to meet with him immediately after my meeting with the imams today and give him a list of Muslim names I am supposed to gather that match the criteria that he has provided."

"You think that he thinks he can ID 6 of 10…is that where you are going with this?" DC asked.

"I am certain of this. What I don't know is what he will do with the information, and I am not sure he'll keep his word and share the killer's motive… which would bring us, that is, the task force and FBI, that much closer to identifying the killer. If he knows who the killer is, well, he isn't cooperating with us. He told me flat out that his interests are serving the best interests of the US government and Army, which means hiding the fact that an American soldier is a serial killer."

"Do you have any thoughts about what he'll do once he has the information?" DC asked.

"I think it entirely plausible for him to set a trap. Neutralize the killer and disappear with her, dead or alive. This would leave the task force investigations open with no possibility of closure for the victims' families. In other words, there wouldn't be any more killings, but the civilian cases would remain open."

"This cowboy isn't after glory, is he? He's not a bounty hunter or anything?"

"Sara told me she did a background on him and confirmed that he is who he says he is, but anything else about him is "protected' information. His file is extremely thin and is only available to people a lot higher up in the food chain than even you, boss, no offense intended."

DC didn't say anything for several minutes. Rainey knew he was thinking about the problem she was facing. It was important to stop the killer, but it was just as important—more important—to protect the life or lives of the five other women the killer was targeting. The list Rainey hoped to produce with the help of the Muslim community might give law enforcement an edge in protecting the killer's targets…here and in other locations the killer might migrate to. Somehow the captain had to be forced to give up the intel he had on the killer. Minutes dragged by. Her boss had put her on hold. Rainey figured he was making some calls that might prove helpful. She waited.

"Rainey?"

"I'm still here." Rainey replied.

"This is what I want you to do. After we hang up I want you to call Sara and tell her about this conversation. You are to make it clear to her that both of you are not to talk to anyone until I give the okay. This includes not talking to the task force and Captain Daniels. Is that clear?"

"Yes, Sir."

"You are to go to your meeting with the Muslim leaders and get as much identifying information as you can from them. You are not, I repeat, not to tell them anything except to explain that learning about the members of the community will help the investigation. You will say that later today or early tomorrow, you could have some information for them which will help them better protect their female family members from becoming victims of the killer. You are not to say any more or less than this. Can you do this?"

"I can, but I don't understand, Sir. There are lives at stake, and I have made it clear that I think the time is short and the killer will strike soon, if we don't act to protect the women we know she is targeting. She *is* targeting one for sure."

"How many times have you heard me scream and holler about how politics will screw up almost any investigation?"

"More times than I can count," Rainey replied with simmering anger in her tone.

"Rainey you need to trust me. Right now what you and the task force need is the cooperation of Captain Daniels with this investigation, right?" Rainey's boss didn't wait for her to respond but continued, "I have to go through the Justice Department, the US Army and Interpol if I am going to get Captain Daniels ordered to cooperate. Do you understand this, Rainey?"

"Yes, Sir." was Rainey's meek reply.

"You have written in your reports that you have a long standing relationship with a Muslim woman named Zarinah Awad. She is trusted by every mosque community and I believe you have full confidence and trust in her. Am I correct?"

"Yes, Sir."

"At your meeting today with her and the imams, you need to create a plan that will have the potential targets at one of the mosques from the time their husbands go to work until their husbands can pick them up. If it is a daughter...then a father, but the women will be in the mosque during the hours the killer has struck in the past. They will not be in their homes or out shopping.

Can you, your friend, and the Muslim leaders concoct some plausible reason for the women to be at the mosque each day for at least a week, or until we have time to track down and apprehend the killer?"

"I think we can come up with something. It can't be as obvious as only the potential targets go to the mosque, and there is a possibility that the killer could show up disguised as a Muslim woman."

"My profile indicates that if in disguise, the killer won't be saying much. If food is not served, the possibility of the killer using poison is eliminated. You and Sara can wear Muslim dress and pretend to be Muslim. It will be your job to make sure the potential targets are not isolated or alone with anyone else at these meetings at any time. You'll need to invent a very plausible reason for the women to be at the mosque every day and all day. This killer is smart and crafty…is able to use innovation and seems to have studied Islamic practices, so make sure everyone acts as normal as possible. Be creative, Rainey."

"I think it might be better not to tell the women. I think the Muslim leaders can persuade the husbands to cooperate without going into a lot of detail. Zarinah and the Muslim leaders will have to work out details."

"Well, we have a plan of sorts for now, Rainey. Anything else?"

"Not sure what to do about today. The killer could strike to-day…this afternoon even," Rainey's voice had that worried tone again.

"Hmmm…" was one of DC's impatient responses.

"We'll figure it out at the meeting today," Rainey said. "I've got to get moving if I am going to be there on time."

"Call me when the meeting is over if I don't call you first. Call Sara as soon as we hang up."

Rainey heard the dial tone. The situation was serious and tense. Waiting for DC to call back, and counting on his being able to force the captain to work with the task force would be difficult. Nothing Rainey could do about that except wait. Rainey made the phone call to Sara and repeated everything she and their boss had discussed per his order. Sara said she would hang out with the task force until she heard again from Rainey.

Rainey locked the house, got in her car, and headed for the mosque to keep her appointment.

Muslim Leaders

Rainey arrived at the mosque about ten minutes early. Zarinah was already there waiting outside for her. Her husband Bibi was standing next to her talking with the armed security guard.

Zarinah greeted her with her an unusually somber salaams.

"Salaams everyone," Rainey replied so she could include the Muslim security guard in her greeting.

Bibi held the front door for his wife and Rainey. In the foyer they took off their shoes and placed them on one of the shelves. "Bibi, I need to talk with Zarinah for a few minutes before we go into the meeting. Is there a room where we can have some privacy?"

"There is the sister's meeting room. Will that do?" Bibi asked, and gave Rainey one of his infectious grins. Bibi always seemed to be happy. *They made a good match when they decided to marry,* Rainey thought, as he opened the door for them and then closed it.

"He'll wait outside until we get through talking then he'll walk us to the main conference room. I called each imam, and they all said they will be here and they have the lists you asked for. You look very serious, Rainey. Something else happened, hasn't it?" Zarinah said and her usually jolly face looked as serious as Rainey's.

Rainey explained about most of what she and DC had discussed except for the details about the political minefield her boss had to transverse. Zarinah was quick to grasp the situation and what was needed.

"At the meeting today we will have the imams call the husbands or responsible males we identify, and the imams will tell them to leave work immediately and go straight home. We will do this before we do anything else... there is such fear in the community that the brothers will do this without question."

"That takes care of today, but we still have to have some plausible reason for the women to come and stay at the mosque until their husbands or families come for them, for a week, or maybe even two," Rainey said.

"We will have a two-week charity drive for the sisters of the advanced English-Arabic classes. They will be fasting during the daytime hours to strengthen their prayer in support of the projects they will be working on to later sell and donate to charity. The women will love this. They can do crafts, sew, knit…and visit while practicing Arabic or English or both! Working in His service for a charitable cause will help take their minds off their fear and they will feel much safer here in the masjid with the armed guards. A few of us older sisters can help babysit the babies and toddlers."

"I think this could work and shouldn't arouse the suspicions of the killer who is probably stalking one or more of the women," Rainey remarked. "The idea of fasting removes the potential danger of anyone eating poisoned food if the killer should somehow manage to get into the mosque. My friend Sara and I will be covered and providing protection inside while the brothers provide it outside the masjid."

"Allah willing, this killer will be caught soon," Zarinah replied and then said a *dua*, or supplication, in Arabic. Rainey waited for her to finish.

"Are we ready to go meet the imams and get them working on contacting the husbands?" Zarinah asked.

I am about as ready as I will ever be to meet eight very learned religious men," Rainey replied, as she opened the door wide so Zarinah's wheelchair could get through the doorway.

Rainey and Zarinah sat at a corner table in the back of the Phoenician drinking raspberry iced tea. They had spent a grueling hour with the imams.

"You should be working at the UN or head up the USA Diplomatic Corps for the Middle East," Rainey said as she grasped Zarinah's hand and gave it a gentle squeeze. "You saved that meeting from total disaster."

"I didn't think there would be any problems with getting the Imams to call the families and get the men to go home immediately. I just hadn't counted on you not providing full information to them, Rainey." Zarinah looked steadily at her friend across the table and watched the conflicting emotions chase across her face.

"I could see your frustration and I appreciate you continuing to use your persuasive abilities to get the imams to check their lists against the list of criteria." Rainey replied carefully. Zarinah could tell that Rainey was still choosing her words carefully.

"You are right. I was just as upset as they were. Every time one of them would try to politely phrase the question of why those names or sisters are being targeted, you were vague and avoided answering directly. We all know that that list means those sisters are possible targets. What we don't know is why or who the serial killer might be…what is the killer's motive besides hate? I think the imams were right to ask you. The families should know the reason."

"I know, Zarinah, and as soon as I can, I will provide the information. Right now the investigation is ongoing. We can't give out too much information. People just naturally talk about something like this, and we don't want the wrong person listening in. If the families panic and begin behaving differently or leave the community as several imams suggested, the killer will know we are getting close and might escape. Good for the sisters on our list and in the communities here, but what about other Muslim communities? This is a large country for the killer to disappear into. If we spook the killer now, we may never solve these cases, and the killer will remain free to continue killing."

"I understand what you are saying, Rainey, but these imams can be trusted." Zarinah was not the least bit mollified.

Rainey sighed. Her tension had only been partially relieved after the imams decided to cooperate. After only twenty minutes, a very short list of ten names was handed to Rainey. Zarinah and the imams had spoken softly in Arabic and Rainey had waited patiently. She resolved that she was going to learn Arabic. Better that, than being left sitting on the outside and having to rely on someone else—even if Zarinah was a great help, there might not always be someone like Zarinah to count on.

Why hasn't the boss called?, she thought. It was already ten minutes after one and she was supposed to meet the captain soon. Sara and the task force were waiting on her to call, also.

"By your silence, I know you will not tell me anything more right now. Can you call Bibi and have him come and pick me up? He has my cell phone with him."

"I'm truly sorry, Zarinah. I had hoped my boss would have called by now. I have to drive to Phoenix now and meet with the task force. As soon as I know something for sure I'll call you. I really appreciate you getting the ball rolling on this safety net for the women. Are you certain each one on the list will go to the mosque tomorrow and every day for the next two weeks and wait there until they get picked up by a family member?"

"The imams will make sure it happens. Don't worry. You and Sara will be there with us each day, and I feel a lot better knowing that."

"Zarinah could you do one last thing for me? Could you check around and see if there are any new single sisters in the community…say within the last six months?"

"Yes…and I know…you will tell me later why you want to know," Zarinah said quietly and without reproach. "Rainey?"

Rainey looked at her friend and waited. She knew Zarinah had something important to say.

"Are you aware that the ten names on the final list are Arab names? The husbands of the three murdered sisters are Iraqi emigrants. The mother of one of those sisters was born in Iraq. All the families are Sunni Muslim. All three sisters and their family members visited in Iraq in the last four years. Four other sisters on the list may have family members from Iraq. Does this help?"

Comprehension of the importance of what Zarinah had just said flashed in Rainey's mind. Iraq…soldiers…USA Army. Rainey bent down and gave Zarinah a big hug. "Yes, my friend, that helps more than you know!"

Bibi arrived to collect his wife. Rainey paid the bill and they left the restaurant. "Salaams, Rainey," Zarinah said, and hugged her. "You be careful, girl. I will be saying duas for Allah to protect you." Zarinah hesitated and then said, " Rainey…the imams believe that the killings have something to do with the war going on in Iraq. They didn't say anything because they thought the police would either ignore them, or accuse them of looking for trouble."

"Thank you Zarinah, and please thank the imams."

Rainey's cell phone remained silent. She got in her car and headed for the freeway and Phoenix headquarters.

The Killer

The killer had had a busy day driving to service stations in the Phoenix metropolitan area to obtain a gallon of gasoline from each for the out-of- gas vehicles she pretended had stranded her. The house and all its contents would burn to the ground tonight, leaving ashes and no trace of her fingerprints or physical evidence for the police slugs to gather.

She looked at the checklist. The cars had been switched early that morning. Her Muslim disguise that would be used the next afternoon, the wig and face mask, were in the trunk of the car with her tools. The small backpack was also tossed into the trunk. The backpack was stuffed with the phony driver's licenses, doctored passports, cash, and bank books for accounts that were established long before she arrived in Mesa and rented a house under an assumed name.

SK held the pillow against the face she saw in the mirror. The face, framed by a natural auburn hair wig was beautiful. But the killer saw something else. She saw a face with an ugly red burn scar puckering the flesh and tuffs of auburn hair sticking out of a partially bald head. Her face was a constant reminder of the deceivers, and seeing her ruined face caused her to relive the horror. She felt suffocated by the acrid smell of her own burning flesh. With an almost animal cry she turned away from the mirror.

SK paced back and forth thinking. She felt uneasy in spite of the careful planning. Nagging thoughts about the three wasted hours in the afternoon, waiting for 6 of 10 to get her brats from school increased the unease. *Why did the husband come home early with the kids?* The killer continued to pace and think about this break in the family routine.

"What is going on? I didn't see any notice that the school was letting out early. Why did the husband come home early today? I don't like it!" the killer screamed her frustration into the mirror. She detested the face that was reflected back. That scar… Killing that black market plastic surgeon in Mexico and torching the records had seemed like a good idea at the time, but now the killer had to live with the botched surgery.

Her anger rekindled and mounted just thinking of the doctor. *He promised! He said he could give me a new head of red-gold hair that would shimmer in the sunlight and move like silk…like the hair I lost in the explosion that killed and crippled my buddies.* The killer screamed again and again, and in a fit of rage, tore the wig off and threw it violently across the room.

It's his own fault he's dead! She picked up the vase from the coffee table and hurled it at the mirror, watching it shatter into small shards that landed at her feet.

She began pacing again as the white noise inside her head increased. She had to be patient and wait for nightfall to torch this house. Only then would she get some relief…decrease the white noise that squeezed her brain and gave such excruciating pain.

6 of 10 was going to die. She would cease to exist. She would die a horrible, painful death with her deceitful face disfigured and her head made bald. If the husband showed up again with the older brats, then they would all die. All but the baby. *The baby can live and suffer like my friends' families.* That thought made the killer smile.

The gallons of gasoline were waiting for the killer. In less than thirty minutes each room was saturated. All that was needed was a lighted match. Chairs, couches, and mattresses were cut and ripped open so the gasoline saturated the material. Doors and drapes were splashed and the carpets soaked. She planned to turn on the stove's gas jets and douse the flames to speed things along. It would be a glorious fire. Her eyes glowed, pulse quickened, and the white noise abated, as she anticipated the excitement of watching the fire department, police, and gawkers arrive to see her handiwork. Maybe she'd try to interview one of the brave firemen? She let loose a hideous laugh.

She picked up the envelope with the words *Agent Walker-FBI* in large letters stenciled on the back of the envelope. She walked out the back kitchen door to sit on the porch and watch the sun go down while waiting for the darkness of night and the fun to begin.

I-SID

Rainey's cell phone rang. She flipped it open and saw that the call was from Sara. Rainey pushed the speaker button and said, "Hi, Sara. I'm enroute to Phoenix headquarters. I got the names with me. Be there in about fifteen minutes. Can't talk as traffic is heavy." She disconnected the call and concentrated on navigating the heavy westbound traffic. Now was not the time for Twenty Questions with Sara.

Rainey drove to the back parking lot and as she parked the car saw Sara sprinting to the car from the back door. *Now what?* Rainey thought. She unlocked the passenger door, and Sara climbed in, slamming the door shut.

"Sara, I am really concerned. I haven't heard from DC and…"

"…and you don't know what to do about Captain Daniels," Sara finished Rainey's sentence and grinned. "You missed the fireworks, Rainey. I was in the task force conference room and we were brainstorming, waiting for you to finish your meeting and get here, when somebody pushed the outside door buzzer and didn't let up on it. Lieutenant Jerald clicked the lock and yanked it open, and Sergeant Ames almost fell through the doorway.

"Seems Captain Daniels just waltzed into Major Billing's reception area in full military uniform…ribbons and brass and all, and dumps four enormous files on Sergeant Ames's desk in front of her. He gives her this really cold look, her words, and orders her to take the files to the task force. He then asks her just as coldly, 'Major Billings in his office?' She said she was dumbfounded and just nodded her head. Then the captain opened the major's door without even knocking. Sergeant Ames told us all she could hear was Major Billings shouting. She lugged the files with her to the task force and that's why she almost fell into the room!" Sara could not stop grinning at Rainey's stunned expression.

"Then Major Billings calls Robert and they talk for about five minutes. After he hangs up he tells the task force members to carry the four files to the murder room and get to work. He tells me that we, the lieutenant and I, are supposed to wait until you arrive and then all three of us are to report to Major Billings' office."

"Wow! DC must have called in an awful lot of markers to get the captain and all his files here," Rainey grinned in response.

"He knew the captain would be showing up here. Probably why he didn't call you, Rainey. Figured you'd find out soon enough."

"Can I see the list before we go inside?" Sara asked.

Rainey nodded and pulled a yellow sheet of notebook paper from her unlocked briefcase and handed it to Sara. "Zarinah told me some information that is really important. She said all the names on the list are connected to Iraq. Either the women or their husbands are originally from Iraq. And there's more. You can read my notes once we get inside the building, Sara."

Sara looked at the list several times. "Oh my God, Rainey, 6 of 10 is probably a member of the Tempe Muslim community!"

Rainey grabbed the paper from Sara to see the name. "We met her at the event. She's about your height, Sara. She is between twenty-two and thirty-five years old, and has two school aged girls and a toddler boy. I signed her daughter's *Hijabi Sisters* books. Her mother still has family living in Iraq. She's second generation

Arab-American born here in the USA, and her husband is a political asylum status emigrant from Iraq. She is the only one on the list meeting all of the criteria of the killer.

"We better get moving, Rainey before they come looking for us. You are not going to believe all the intel the captain withheld from us," Sara said as they began walking towards the elevator.

"We've got a big problem though. Not even the captain knows what our killer looks like today. I'll let the captain explain why. Let's get upstairs and get the meeting with the major over with so we can get back with the task force members and you can see the new profile in the murder room that we now have of this psycho. Rainey, she's really gone off the deep end. She's smart and crazy like a fox."

Rainey and Sara went to the conference room first to give the task force members the information gleaned from the imams. The task force could begin work creating a strategy on how best to protect 6 of 10, an ex-Iraqi named Amel and her family, while the lieutenant, Rainey and Sara went to meet with Major Billings and the captain in the major's office.

Lieutenant Jerald buzzed them into the conference room and shook Rainey's hand. "Good work, Agent Walker. I suppose your partner has filled you in on some of the intel that came from the reluctant Captain Daniels?"

"I gave her an overview about what's been going on here this afternoon, but didn't have time to go into the new killer profile and the motive intel," Sara said.

"Lieutenant Jerald, do you think I could take about ten minutes to look at the new profile of the killer?" Rainey asked.

"Hold on. I'll let the major know you are here and that we'll report to his office in about fifteen minutes. He can send Sergeant Ames to collect the information you got from the mosque leaders. It will give him some time to look over it before we meet with him and the captain."

"Just make sure he doesn't let the captain leave his office. Once he has that information, I wouldn't put it past him to try a lone ranger act, disappear again, and go after the killer by himself," Rainey said, and she was serious. The lieutenant was serious, too, when he nodded his understanding.

Rainey and Sara walked around the partition and were greeted by a chorus of hellos from the SKTF. This time around, Rainey was certain their smiles and welcomes were sincere. She didn't feel her usual aversion to a murder room and was anxious to get up to speed.

Detective Ramirez touched Rainey lightly on the arm to gain her attention and held out a folder that housed Captain Daniels' profile of the killer. Officer White handed her a second slender folder that summarized a profile for each of the newly discovered victims of their serial killer. Rainey glanced at the Victim Profile board and was shocked to see so many new photographs pinned to the board. As she read each summary she looked at the victims' photos. Rainey's anger grew as she realized that Captain Daniels and his supervisors had withheld so much information. She was also, deep down, angry and disappointed in the person the captain actually was. He had almost derailed the SKTF investigation and used everyone he came into contact with.

Rainey took a deep breath and buried her anger, for now. She needed to read the files and didn't have much time. She read the summary sheets the task force prepared:

Ten-Count Victim 1

- *Corporal Harold Summers, New Mexico Army Reserves; Military ID # 29356604*
- *Active Duty Service in Iraq: April 2004 – July 2005*
- *Assignment: Mechanic and Security*
- *Active Duty Service in Bosnia: September 2005 – November 2005*

- *Assignment: Mechanic and Security*
- *Returned to USA from active duty 11/15/2006 and returned to civilian job*
- *DOB: 3/12/1972*
- *Height: 5'6"*
- *Weight: 170 lbs.*
- *Social Security 444-34-8010*
- *Residence: Gallup, N. Mexico*
- *Single*
- *Parents both deceased; No siblings*
- *Employed by Uni-Tec in Gallup N. Mexico for 6 years.*
- *Failed to show up for work 12/01/2006*
- *Missing person report filed with Gallup PD a week later by supervisor and friend*
- *Known acquaintance of prime suspect; served together in Iraq and Bosnia.*
- *Part of a Platoon that was attacked by a suicide bomber; was on guard duty and not in attack location.*
- *Psychological profile: Guilt for not being with his buddies when attacked. PTSD discharge after incident in Bosnia.*
- *Unprovoked assault on a Muslim male.*
- *About a year (2007) after Summers' disappearance, body found in a shallow grave in Arizona desert –Yuma.*
- *Neck broken-spinal cord severed – See ME's report*
- *Yellow Post-it note left with the body-Text: Coward-Collateral Damage.*
- *Assumption based on note left by the killer: Cpl. Summers*

refused to go along with the suspect's plans to kill the Muslim women, became a threat to suspect, murdered by suspect. Summers' bank accounts closed and all monies withdrawn either by Summers or killer.

Ten-Count Victim 2 (03/18/2007)

- Eduardo Calles Garcia Cordoba
- Doctor-surgeon: plastic surgery-retired
- Juarez Mexico
- DOB: 04/07/1942
- Height: 5' 8" Weight: 210 Brown/Brown
- Residence: Juarez Mexico
- Wife deceased, no living children
- Known Escobedo Cartel ties: drugs; medical services to cartel; practiced medicine-black market activities.
- Cordoba's body was found in the ashes-debris of torched building where Cordoba conducted his black market surgeries; identified by dental records
- Cause of fire: definitely arson; all records/files presumed destroyed in the fire.
- Cause of death: .22 caliber; 2 shots, (1) right temple, (2) heart; bullets recovered
- Type of ammo the killer used---**See Ballistics report
- Interview by Mexican police with Margarita Jimenez-medical assistant/receptionist (03/20/2007)
- Day of fire Cordoba had one patient female: had previously performed plastic surgery on face and breast area of patient: burn scarring; Jimenez stated that the patient also had hair transplants, but regrowth failed; patient identified from

military medical photos to be Lieutenant Elaine Alice Stewart –US Army Reserves status AWOL; whereabouts unknown since her return from Bosnia active duty (11/15/2006

- *Witness did not see the suspect after the bandages from surgery were removed—told not to go into work that day. Same day doctor killed and place of business torched.*

**Note→ Recovered bullet is a Black Talon: a hollow point manufactured by Winchester. Winchester stopped manufacturing this bullet in 1993. The bullet is designed to make a small entry wound, but when the bullet penetrates the copper jacket peels open to form a six-point star. The tips of each star point are razor sharp and are designed to do maximum damage. Some of this ammo is still in circulation, but generally can only be obtained through the black market or possibly in military channels overseas.

Rainey closed the file and leaned back in the chair and rubbed her eyes. Her eyes felt gritty and ached from lack of sleep. She was bone tired. Rainey intended to read each of the case files thoroughly, but for now the file summaries helped fill in some of the blanks.

Two other folders contained summaries of the first two female Muslim victims and the case files. Rainey had already gone through the redacted case files in Captain Daniels' temporary office. She would need to read the non-redacted originals.

With the four known Ten-Count victims, three Scarf Killer victims, and the murder of Sergeant Williams, the serial killer had murdered eight people—maybe more—and intended to kill five more Muslim women. The killer had shown that she would kill anyone perceived to be a threat to her plan. Rainey stood and stretched while her mind reeled at the enormity of the loss of life and the cunning and savagery of the serial killer. Members of the task force had often called the killer a psycho. Rainey felt there was a lot of truth in that label and was anxious to hear what Captain Daniels had to say about Lieutenant Elaine Stewart.

Lieutenant Jerald walked into the murder room. "It's time to meet with Major Billings and Captain Daniels, Rainey."

"Okay," she replied. "I didn't have time to look at Captain Daniels' reports. Is there information in those reports indicating the motive for the killer selecting specifically named Muslim women and not targeting and killing just any Muslim woman? After reading the summary of the fourth Ten-Count victim, Dr. Cordoba, I am assuming the killer's burns and disfigurement are central to the killer's motive."

"I'll let Captain Daniels brief you on this, Rainey. It's a real horror story," Lieutenant Jerald stated, as he and Rainey left the task force office.

Sara was waiting for them at the elevator with two cans of diet cola. "Ready?" Sara asked as she handed Rainey one of the cans. Rainey took the can and gave Sara a grateful smile. The elevator door opened and the three law enforcement officers stepped into the elevator.

Motive

Lieutenant Jerald, Rainey, and Sara walked into the reception office and said hello to Sergeant Ames. She pressed the intercom and said, "Sir, the lieutenant and the two FBI agents are here."

"Send them in," Major Billings' voice came through the intercom.

When Rainey entered the major's office she saw the major seated at the head of a conference desk. Captain Daniels was seated to his right. The captain gave Rainey a cold, hard look and stayed seated. His posture was stiff, and he didn't bother to acknowledge anyone.

"Have a seat everyone. Thanks for coming in. I understand all of you had little sleep last night and have been working non-stop. Now that we are here together, perhaps we can put politics and agency differences aside and work together to catch this killer before she kills anyone else."

Everyone nodded their acceptance of the major's conciliatory words except the captain, who remained unsmiling and remote.

"Before we get into some nuts and bolts of how to go forward, I'd like to hear from Captain Daniels the motive of this killer, and why she is only targeting specific Muslim women. I haven't had time to read through the complete investigation reports of Captain Daniels. What was previously shared with me was extremely redacted, and from what I know now, a lot of critical intel was missing." Rainey tried her best to sound civil, but everyone in the room heard the anger resonating in her words.

Major Billings looked from Rainey to the captain seated across the table from her. They looked like they were ready to go to war with each other. He cleared his throat to buy some time.

Daniels tossed a file across the table and it landed in front of Rainey. The relief on the major's face was apparent to Sara, who had been watching Rainey and the captain to see which one went on the attack first. *One point for Rainey,* Sara thought as she settled into her seat. At this meeting, about all she would be doing is listening.

"You can follow along with my report or read it later, Agent Walker," Captain Daniels' words were clipped and very professional. Rainey just nodded her head and didn't say anything.

"In August of 2004, Lieutenant Elaine Alice Stewart, US Army Reserves, was on her first tour of active duty in Iraq. Lieutenant Stewart was a nurse in her civilian life, and was attending courses to become qualified as a surgical nurse. She was assigned to one of the Army's moving medical field hospitals as a medical corpsman. Lieutenant Stewart is single—never married, no children, no siblings, and both parents are deceased. She is five feet nine inches in height and her consistent normal weight is 130 pounds, blue eye color, and auburn-colored shoulder length hair. Lieutenant Stewart was physically fit. Stateside, she worked out in a gym and jogged every day.

"Her connection to Arizona is her mother's sister who lived in Mesa. Lieutenant Stewart often spent summers and vacations as a teenager with her aunt. Her aunt is deceased and the home was sold and is a furnished rental property. The house is currently vacant. The last tenant moved out about four months ago.

"In a small village forty clicks north of downtown Baghdad, the Army had assigned a platoon, four squads of seven soldiers each, with two squads of mortar and artillery soldiers, to rebuild the town's school and medical clinic. Lieutenant Steward was on loan for this important project and was deployed to this area to work. She worked with the local Iraqi medics and gave assistance as needed to the platoon soldiers.

The platoon set up camp outside the town. There were living quarters, a chow hall tent, latrines, and a medical tent. The soldiers took all their meals separately in the chow tent. Orders were to be friendly, but not mix with the locals outside of the work hours.

On November 30, 2004 two of the platoon squads and one mortar squad were in the chow hall for the midday meal. Lieutenant Stewart had been to the latrine and was approaching the chow hall. Corporal Summers, one of the victims in the Ten-Count investigation, was changing the tires on a jeep parked within a few feet of the chow hall. There was a huge explosion inside the chow hall tent. Ten good men were torn to pieces by the work of a suicide bomber, a local serving food to the soldiers. The remaining soldiers, all eleven, were seriously injured, burned, lost limbs or sight and hearing. It was a bloody hell slaughter!" Captain Daniels' voice shook with his inner rage at this act of violence. He grabbed the glass of water in front of him and drained it.

Rainey gulped and felt as if she could not breathe. The others in the room remained silent and waited for the captain to regain his composure. They all looked away from him to give what limited privacy they could.

"Corporal Summers' injuries were not life threatening, being shielded by being behind the closed jeep. He found Lieutenant Stewart on the ground about ten feet from where the chow tent had been pitched. She was conscious and trying to standup. Her hair was burnt to the skull and she had suffered a burn injury to the chest area from flying debris. His report on the terrorist attack stated that Lieutenant Stewart grabbed the corporal's baseball cap from his head to cover her injuries and took his jacket, put it on, and zipped it to hide her wound. Then she insisted he help her as she moved into what was left of the tent to begin treating the injured. Reports stated that she worked over twenty-four hours without sleep or treatment. Even after medical help arrived, she insisted on staying on duty until every last soldier was taken care of. Only then did she seek medical care for her own injuries. Her heroism is unquestioned by the US Army, and we honored her for the lives she saved that day."

The captain's voice had grown softer and he looked as if he had been sucker punched. He paused for a minute, as if honoring the memory of the soldiers who had died and the memory of the person who Lieutenant Stewart had once been.

"Most of the injured were flown to Germany for treatment, but Lieutenant Stewart insisted, and persuaded the brass that she could recover and finish her tour of duty. She saw all the shrinks and was certified as fit for duty once her chest burn healed over. There wasn't much that could be done about the scarring on her scalp. She started wearing a short brown wig when she returned to active status."

"While she was in recovery, she worked in administration in the Baghdad Command Center. She asked to be assigned to work in records, doing filing and processing reports." Captain Daniels paused to pour another glass of water and drink half its contents before continuing.

"What I say next, and I note this in my investigation reports, is based on deductive reasoning and logical assumptions given all I, we, have learned about Lieutenant Stewart's life since the day of the explosion.

"The reports of the investigation into the explosion, identifying the suicide bomber and the organization responsible for providing the explosives came into Baghdad Central, and were reviewed before being sent Stateside. The reports turned up a list of ten possible suspects to find and to interrogate."

"The Arab names," Rainey spoke aloud without realizing it.

Captain Daniels looked at Rainey and said without a bit of warmth in his voice, "Yes, the names you got today match some of the names on the terror suspect list. The Army believes that Lieutenant Stewart copied the investigation reports to target very specific female Muslim victims."

"So our scarf killer doesn't intend to kill just any Muslim female?" Sara asked.

"Her victims are within a certain age range...the same age range as the soldiers who were killed in the explosion. They're Arab or have Arab husbands, have one of the names on her Ten-List, and either she, her husband, or a family member must have lived in Iraq."

Lieutenant Jerald spoke up, "Lieutenant Stewart has been exhibiting personality and character traits of most serial killers. Taking the lives of ten Muslim women for the lives of the ten soldiers killed that day. Same methodology. Careful planning. Arrogance and the belief that her skills and abilities are superior to law enforcement."

"The Post-it notes, making sure we know the work is hers and nobody else's," Sara added.

"My sincere condolences, Captain Daniels, on the loss of the soldiers in Iraq. I understand why you tried to keep a lot of information from becoming part of the Scarf Killer investigations. Lieutenant Stewart is still US Army, she's AWOL, and she's a dangerous and psychotic serial killer who must be caught and stopped. But I don't believe there is any way you can keep your investigation separate, and you shouldn't you have tried. She is the killer in both investigations, and now she's also a cop killer," Rainey said.

Captain Daniels did not attempt to rebut Rainey's comments.

Sara spoke up again and asked, "I think we can safely assume that the killer's cutting off of her victims' hair are acts of revenge for her own hair loss and the targets are Muslim females because the suicide bomber was a Muslim woman?"

"That is a fair assumption and my conclusion," the captain replied.

"What isn't clear to me is why she killed Corporal Summers. After she finished her tour in Iraq, she came home, and then was deployed to Bosnia. Corporal Summers was also deployed at the same time to Bosnia. Isn't it reasonable to assume that they remained friends?"

"I have had to make more assumptions which may or may not be fact, but they seem logical. The only way we will ever really know is if Lieutenant Stewart admits to them," replied Captain Daniels. "The first female victim was killed in Iraq, the 1 of 10 victim. The second victim was killed over a year later in Bosnia, 2 of 10. Both Summers and Stewart were in the country when the killings took place. We do have the report of the Corporal's unprovoked assault on a Muslim male in Bosnia. No weapons were used, and the victim was not permanently injured. It shows a tendency the corporal may have had to hate Muslims, but it is not proof of psychosis. One possibility is that Summers and Stewart were both involved in the first two murders."

"Your report stated that this was a possibility, but you believed Lieutenant Stewart to have acted alone in both those killings," Major Billings commented.

"Right. From all his evaluations, Summers seemed to have weathered the PTSD phase. He was doing well in recovery and getting back into his civilian life. There was nothing to indicate he had gone off the deep end, until he went AWOL about the same time Stewart went AWOL. The other male suspect I was tracking down was found in a commune in Colorado. He is another PTSD victim who is now in Walter Reed Hospital getting treatment."

"It's possible that Stewart confided in Summers, or he might have discovered it on his own and confronted her? No one remembers seeing her at his place of business or apartment in Gallup, according to your reports," Sara commented

"Maybe he became collateral damage for Stewart in her twisted mind, and she used his death to distract the investigation. You used your personnel, resources, and time trying to find him, and he was a prime suspect until his body was discovered and identified," Lieutenant Jerald pointed out.

Captain Daniels looked thoughtful and took his time responding. "I think where Corporal Summers is concerned, we'll have to give him the benefit of the doubt and stick with Stewart acting alone in all the killings, but this may very well be one element of the case we won't be able to answer for a certainty."

"Robert, any news on whether the email correspondence between Sergeant Williams and the killer might help us locate the killer?" Sara asked.

"Both ISPs were very helpful. The killer established a bank account under a phony name, and we assume that she used a phony ID to setup the ISP. The morning of the murder, the killer closed the bank account and ISP service. The hard drive was taken from the sergeant's computer but we found some printed email messages that identified which ISP the sergeant used. The killer played him big time," Lieutenant Jerald said. He shook his head and had to tamper down his anger. Getting angry just got in the way of logical thinking. This killer was very smart and always several steps ahead of the task force.

Rainey's cell phone vibrated and she flipped the cover and saw it was Zarinah calling. "Excuse me for a minute. I need to answer this phone call." Rainey got up from the table and created some space between her and the others in the room so her conversation would not disrupt their discussion.

"Salaams, Zarinah. Yes, I am meeting with the task force supervisors and others involved in the investigation." Rainey remained silent for several minutes as Zarinah talked rapidly without pausing.

"You did the best you could, Zarinah. I know they are afraid. I understand that completely. This killer is extremely dangerous, and they should be very concerned. Yes, the killer's next target is one of those five Muslim sisters. Sister Amel. Okay. Stay where you are. Tell those with you to stay put. Nobody is to leave and nobody, absolutely nobody is to be allowed inside. I'll tell the task force commander and call you back shortly. Love you too."

Rainey closed her cell phone cover and walked back to the table. She wasn't sure how Zarinah's news would be received, but it sure limited the possibilities for setting up a trap.

"At the meeting today with the Muslim leaders, I had a tough time convincing them not to push the panic button. They called the husbands and asked them to go home so their wives would not be alone and unprotected. They agreed to wait on my phone call after I came back here to see what plan would be developed for long-term protection until the killer was caught. A tentative plan was to have the families go to the mosque tomorrow and stay there an indeterminate number of days and nights. Zarinah and her husband stayed at the mosque with the leaders.

"Since the community event the other day, word was spread to watch for anything unusual, like people in the neighborhood who don't live there, or somebody taking pictures. They were also told to report if anyone felt like they were being followed as they went about their usual activities.

"An elderly woman living with her son's family just two houses away from Amel Abdullah was listening to her son talk about the precautions the Muslims are taking. She told her son that a car with a veiled sister just sitting in it, was parked twice a day on that street. This sister doesn't get out of the car and parks in a couple different places along the street. She said what got her to notice this car and Muslim woman is that the car showed up before all the kids went to school and then it showed up when the kids got home from school. The first week this sister started showing up, she would stay in the car, sitting for sometimes over an hour, but in the last couple of days, she's only hung around for ten or fifteen minutes after the mother and kids leave the house and then again when they return. She told her son that today, the Muslim woman didn't show up, and that's why she was thinking so much about this."

"We need to get a female officer over to contact this woman to describe the woman and the car," Lieutenant Jerald said excitedly.

Rainey put up her left hand in a stopping motion. "It won't do any good. The son got as much information as the woman is able to give. The woman in the driver's seat was veiled and her hands were covered, which is an appropriate way for veiled Muslim women to dress. The old woman's eye sight isn't all that good, and she knows nothing about vehicles except to say that she thinks it had two doors not four, and the car was a dark color."

Major Billings said excitedly in a low voice, "The killer, if it was the killer, changed her pattern today. Something is happening."

"I need to tell you what else Zarinah told me," Rainey said, and got everyone's attention again.

"The son called the imam at the Tempe mosque. The leaders talked about this, and decided that the female Muslims on the list and all their family members would come to the Tempe mosque and stay there until the killer is caught. They have two armed guards outside the front and back doors to the mosque and two armed guards stationed on the inside at each door. No one else will be permitted inside the mosque.

"I don't think rent-a-cops are any match for Stewart. She's a fully combat trained soldier," Captain Daniels said.

"One of them is a Phoenix police officer who asked for an emergency family leave just a couple of hours ago. Two others served in Afghanistan and are National Guard," Rainey stated before continuing.

"There aren't any windows on the ground floor and the second floor windows are too high to reach without a long ladder. The mosque has a nursery, library, full-sized kitchen with a freezer, refrigerator, and fully stocked pantry. There are two restrooms, each with a shower. The men will be sleeping in the downstairs community room, and all the women and children in the upstairs prayer room.

Zarinah said the mothers will home-school the children and use the Internet to contact teachers for lessons. They intend to stay inside the mosque for as long as it takes, which is the exact wording the imams told Zarinah to tell me to tell the Phoenix police.

"There goes the possibility of trapping the killer at the victim's house!" exclaimed Sara.

Major Billing's door flew open and Sergeant Ames rushed into the room. "Sorry sir, but this can't wait."

Five pairs of eyes turned towards the opened door and the out-of-breath sergeant. Sergeant Ames was waving one of those message notes in her hand, put it on the table and slid it down the table to the major.

The major stood so abruptly he knocked his chair over. "Everyone to the task force conference room, now. Detective Ramirez needs us there immediately."

Sergeant Ames's mouth fell open. She hadn't ever seen the major move with such speed.

"Rodriguez thinks he's confirmed the location where the killer has been hiding out."

"Confirmed?' four voices said as they hurried behind the major making a beeline for the elevator.

"Sergeant Ames, put in a call to the arson task force and get them headed to the fire location. Get the chief on the phone for me. Then call the Phoenix Fire Chief and have him stay on the line if I'm talking to the chief. He'll need to coordinate the fire investigation with the Mesa Fire Department. Lieutenant Jerald, call Joe…yes…the Patrol Bureau Chief. We need to get some of our Phoenix officers out to the site to help protect the scene." Sergeant Ames kept nodding her head and handed the major the cell phone she was holding. "Chief, we have us an emergency. I need your help."

Everyone piled out of the elevator and raced for the SKTF door that opened before they reached it.

Captain Daniels spoke first, "Detective Ramirez how...who confirmed this house fire location as the place where the killer has been hiding out?"

Detective Rodriguez handed Captain Daniels a copy of a fax. He handed a copy to Lieutenant Jerald, who was talking on his cell phone, and handed copies to Rainey and Sara.

"When that fax came into the office from the Mesa sergeant at the house fire site, Officer White recognized the address because it's in the Ten-Count investigation files Captain Daniels brought in. It's the house that was owned by the killer's aunt. It's supposed to be empty and advertised for lease with the agent."

Rainey interrupted, "This letter the Mesa sergeant faxed here. Where'd he get it?" Rainey demanded.

"I got his cell phone number. He's at the fire scene. Says you can call him." Detective Ramirez handed Rainey a scrap of paper with a phone number written on it.

"The second page of the fax looks like an envelope with the name Agent Rainey Walker—FBI block lettered on it," remarked Sara.

Officer White spoke up, "The killer left you a Post-it note message stuck to the mail box by the front fence, Agent Walker."

"She-the killer did what?" stuttered Captain Daniels.

Officer White said, "The note said a letter was inside the mailbox, and that if Agent Walker crossed her path again, that she would become collateral damage."

Rainey was only half listening. She was absorbed in the one-page letter the killer left inside the mailbox for her:

Agent Walker—or do you mind if I address you as Rainey?

Rainey,

It's a little warmer than usual this Arizona evening. In my other life I am sure we could have jogged together in the mornings and shared some raspberry iced tea and hummus at the Phoenician. You would have liked the person I was. She is dead…killed by a terrorist.

There are dozens of Muslim deceivers in the world who need to die, and I'll find mine, Rainey. I'm good at what I do, and you and that task force won't be able to stop me.

A life for a life, and ten lives were blown apart by a stranger. The Muslim world will forfeit ten of their own by a stranger. I will exact Justice. I can't be stopped from my mission. This is your warning, Rainey. Stay out of my life. You won't like what will happen if you don't.

The letter was left unsigned.

Rainey looked up and saw everyone in the room looking at her. She almost felt guilty, but she didn't know why she should suddenly feel like this. The killer was gone. They didn't even know what she looked like or where to begin looking again. She could walk right by Rainey, and Rainey would be none the wiser. Rainey's legs felt weak, and she grabbed a chair and sat down heavily.

"Robert, I want you and three of task force members to get a chopper ride over to the crime scene in Mesa. Evening traffic is a mess, and I don't want you sitting on the freeway. You need to get there and collect evidence and interview the witnesses. I want the neighbor who reported the fire flown back to headquarters. Is that clear? Do what it takes to make it happen, and call me when you get to the crime scene, but don't stick around. Just make sure you are noticed," ordered Major Billings. "Sara, your boss wants you to phone him ASAP," he added.

"Officer White and Sergeant Ramirez, I want both of you to remain here at the SKTF office and coordinate anything your commander needs, understood?" the major ordered. Both looked disappointed to have to miss out on any action, but nodded at the major and went back into the murder room to man the phones.

Strategy

Captain Daniels hadn't stopped pacing since he was handed the fax. He had a brooding look on his face and his eyes were hard. When the major seemed to be out of orders, the captain stopped pacing.

Rainey was pulling out her cell phone to call Zarinah when she noticed the captain stop, hesitate for a few seconds, and then look at the conference room door before he began to walk towards it.

"Where do you think you are going, Captain?" The major's voice held a sharp edge to it.

Sara and Rainey both looked up and watched the major and captain face off.

Major Billings sat down at the head of the conference table and pointed at the empty chairs around it and said, "You three have a seat."

Captain Daniels exclaimed angrily, "I showed up at your office. I brought you complete copies of my investigative reports. I have conferred with your task force and co-operated with your FBI partners. I've done everything I was ordered to do." The captain threw the copy of the fax he was given on the conference table, placed his hands on the top of the chair and leaned in towards the major. "I'm out of here, Major, and a good evening to you and the ladies," he said mockingly while nodding at Rainey and Sara.

"I asked you politely to sit at the table, Captain. Don't make me call your superior and have him order you to do so," the major snapped back.

Slowly, comprehension dawned on Rainey. Major Billings and the captain didn't buy the killer's goodbye message to her.

The captain hesitated, seemed to get whatever was driving him under control and sat down. His eyes never broke contact with the major's.

Sara and Rainey sat down and waited again to see what these two strong-willed men would say or do next. Rainey slipped her cell phone back into her pocket.

"Do I look like a fool? Do you think the Chief of Police of the Phoenix Police Department wants to look like a fool? He turned his steady gaze on Sara and Rainey, "Do you think your boss, DC Britt—the best serial killer profiler in this nation—is a fool?"

Sara looked across at Rainey and saw that she had already clicked on where the major was going and why Captain Daniels was hell bent on leaving.

"Let's do a short debriefing, and then I'll ask a question." The major held up his hand, indicating the two FBI agents and the US Army SID Investigator should remain silent. He started, lifting one finger for each fact, "One. The killer has destroyed any evidence we might have recovered from the house she has been staying in. I know you checked the house, Captain Daniels. She's smart and planned it that way.

"Two. She left a letter and a Post-it for Agent Walker so we'd know she set the fire and wouldn't be returning.

"Three. She wants us to believe she has given up on her target victim she refers to as 6 of 10.

"Four. We don't know what she looks like now, but we know she has to wear a wig when she is not disguised as a female Muslim.

"Five. We know she has financial resources and is able to obtain phony documents and IDs.

"Six. We know she stopped watching the house of the target victim today.

"Seven. We know she has been in close proximity of Rainey at the mosque and when Rainey was jogging. Possibly at other times and places.

"Eight. We know she will kill anyone she perceives as a threat to her plans.

"Nine. We know she can and has killed two men: one a police officer using a knife, and one using a .22 caliber revolver, and was just as brutal killing the men as she had the women.

"Ten. She has killed one victim at night and the others in daylight hours. We cannot assume she will only kill her female victims during daylight hours.

"Eleven. We know she has used poison, a knife, and a .22 caliber gun to kill her victims.

"Twelve. We know that she thinks she is smarter than the task force and the FBI. She taunts us with her notes.

"Thirteen. We know she is reasonably attractive as Sergeant Williams was flattered by her praise and compliments.

"Fourteen. She has posed as a media reporter and I am certain she is posing as a reporter at the house she torched this evening.

"Fifteen. I think she intends to leave our geographic area, but not until she has killed her target.

"Captain Daniels, Agents Walker and James, do you think our killer has given up and has left the Phoenix metro area to hunt and stalk elsewhere?"

Rainey was the first to respond, "I think she torched the house to draw the task force and FBI to the scene in Mesa. I think she is right now driving to the location where she intends to wait until Amel and her family go to bed and then she will strike. She may intend to kill the entire family."

Sara nodded and said, "I agree. She didn't stalk her victim today so as far as she knows, her victim will be at home with her family and they will be in bed asleep tonight."

"Captain Daniels?" the major asked, as the captain had not said a word, and just seemed to be waiting like a caged tiger.

"You've thought all along that she wasn't leaving town until she went after her target, didn't you? Didn't you!" Rainey's voice matched the fury on her face. "Still playing the lone ranger aren't you?" she stated disgustedly.

"There is no way the military or government can keep this under wraps, even if you did locate her and take her back to a military base, Captain Daniels. Agent Walker's boss made that very clear to your superiors."

Rainey felt drained and disappointed. She watched silently with Sara and Major Billings, as the captain's emotions waged war with his intellect.

The desk phone rang and startled the four law enforcement officers. Major Billings answered the phone. "Okay. Yes. I think we are about ready to come up with a plan. Okay, five minutes, as time is running out."

The major put the phone down. "Lieutenant Jerald and two of the task force members have just landed on the heliport on the roof. They will rejoin us in five minutes. Are you ready to work with us, Captain?"

"If I don't I agree, I suppose you'll have me restrained tonight and turn me over to the US Army in the morning? You'll put me on a plane and make sure the plane leaves Phoenix? Is that pretty much the alternative?"

The major just gave the captain a hard stare without responding.

"I'm in," he finally said.

The conference room door buzzed, and Sergeant Ames came around the partition from the murder room, took a visual cue from the major and opened the door.

"Sergeant Ames, tell Detective Ramirez and Officer White to go to the conference room next door. Our witness is waiting there to be interviewed." Lieutenant Jerald handed her an evidence bag that had the killer's original letter and Post-it note inside. "Log this in as evidence and lock it in the safe until we can get it to P&E in the morning," he told the Sergeant. "Traffic is snarled on the Sixty and all major city streets westbound from Mesa. Our killer is most likely caught up in a traffic jam if she's driving that way. The AZ DPS closed one westbound traffic lane to slow things down for us.

"We just may have time to get people in place before she gets to Tempe and sets up surveillance in the target's neighborhood," the major said.

"The 6 of 10 target...I mean Mrs. Abdullah...isn't at home. She and her family are locked up safe in the Tempe mosque with the other families from the list," Sara reminded everyone.

"But the husband's car is parked in the mosque parking lot with the other vehicles belonging to the families who were also on that list the Muslim leaders put together," said the captain.

The three men in the room as if on cue all looked at Sara. "What?" she said a tad defensively.

Instead of answering Sara, the captain sort of nodded his head and asked Lieutenant Jerald, "Is the parking lot large enough to land the chopper safely?"

"Nope, but the ASU football field is a few blocks from the mosque," Lieutenant Jerald replied.

"It's worth a shot. She has either planned to break into the house in the early morning hours before daylight and take out the entire family, or wait till morning and watch for the husband and kids to leave the house. If they don't leave, she'll put on her disguise, approach the house and try to gain entry using some plausible reason. She's mad and she'll want to make a big statement by slaughtering everyone in the family, because we got too close to her," Captain Daniels said out loud, as if he were talking to himself.

Rainey could see where they were going with their planning and said, "We can get the husband's car, drive to the house and wait. She won't know we're inside waiting for her. She'll see the car parked in the carport and watch the house lights go out. She'll bide her time till she's ready to strike."

"Rainey and I can get some head scarves, those outer robes, and face covers from the women inside the mosque. Rainey can call Zarinah, who is waiting inside, and she can get the clothing and keys to the house and car for us," said Sara.

"The captain can drive the car and wait inside with us while Robert works with the task force outside the house in the neighborhood," said Rainey.

The major interrupted the discussion at this point and said, "If the killer arrives like we think she will, and the neighborhood and outer perimeter are crawling with task force members, she is bound to spot one or more and get spooked. We could lose this chance to stop her and she might just move on, as she said in that damn letter she wrote to Agent Walker."

"I could take the outer perimeter and Lieutenant Jerald can take the inner with Sara," the captain suggested.

Rainey thought she must have missed something…he said Sara and the lieutenant would be the inner perimeter. *What about my position?* she thought.

Major Billings cut her off before Rainey could get a word out. "Time is short, Rainey. There's no time to argue this. Your shoulder hasn't completely healed, and I'm not sending you in with the others. I'd be negligent, and your boss would have my head."

Rainey was furious to be left behind and she stood up and got ready to go at it with the major.

The major raised his voice, just a bit…enough to get her attention. "You are staying here. I've got an important job for you that no one else can do. You have come into contact with our killer at least once. Sara, at any time when you were with Rainey, did you notice any woman wearing a wig? She'd have to be similar in height to our suspect. You've got to go get suited up with body armor, and the three of you on your way to the mosque. You can call her if you remember something. Rainey, call your friend at the mosque and tell her what you need, so she can have everything ready when the chopper sets down in the ASU football field. It's just a few blocks from the mosque, and a Tempe police officer will be waiting to drive the three of you to the mosque. I'll arrange for this as soon as you three get moving."

"So what's this important job I am going to be doing that no one else can do?" Rainey asked sarcastically. She was steamed over being left behind.

"It's just possible that we are too late, or the killer gets spooked, or anything could have happened and our killer has taken a hike like she said. We could have miscalculated, and she could be driving out of state right now to New Mexico, Texas, California, or Colorado. She could even sitting at the airport waiting for a flight to any of dozens of destinations."

Each of the men and women in the room nodded in agreement. What the major said was sobering. Rainey sat down, her arguments silenced. She waited for him to continue.

"Our killer isn't as smart as she thinks she is. Her letter as good as told us that you, and maybe Sara, saw her, maybe spoke to her. There is something that makes her feel this connection to you. She would have had to been wearing a wig, and from the story your boss told me, Sara knows wigs, right? You've seen photos of the killer's face before she had surgery and one thing doesn't change…the shape of the head, the bones…and that's what you are expert in…and drawing faces of suspects, victims, and witnesses from recollection, right?"

Rainey nodded her head as she understood now where he was coming from.

"If she slips through this trap or is already gone, we need a face. We need something to get out to all law enforcement. A face to put out to the media. We need to slow her down and make things as hard as we can for her."

The lieutenant, Sara, and Captain Daniels were headed for the conference room door. "Radio contact at all times. Use the same scrambled frequency and make sure your cell phones are charged or pick up some replacements. Remember, Captain. This is a team effort."

The captain paused and said, "Don't worry about me. I'm on the team and I won't risk the operation or anyone."

"That's what I need to hear," the major said.

Rainey took out her phone and dialed Zarinah. She gave Sara the "V" sign for victory and watched them walk out the door. *God, please watch over my friend and the other two officers,* Rainey prayed silently. She would ask Zarinah to have the Muslims at the mosque pray for the officers, too.

The Killer

She stood about in the center of the large group of media taking pictures of the firemen, police, bystanders, and the house gorgeously engulfed in flames. When the roof began to cave in, she inched her way to the fringes of the group while keeping an eye on the Mesa police sergeant who was moving the neighbor who found the letter and Post-it to a police car.

Where were they? The task force and Agent Walker should have arrived by now. She couldn't wait to capture the look on Rainey's face when she read the letter and her Post-it warning. She wanted a picture of this as a trophy to savor and relive this fantastic moment.

She looked at the road beyond the milling crowd and emergency service vehicles, and saw the red and blue flashing lights coming closer. *Ah…the troops have arrived*, she thought, and her tension and excitement mounted, as the flames rose higher in the evening sky, casting an orange and yellow glow over the faces of the onlookers.

She watched as the doors on the two police vehicles opened with four male officers with task force windbreakers get out and head for the Mesa police sergeant and his witness.

Rage and disappointment welled up inside the killer. She could barely control her shaking hands as she put the camera in its case and moved away from the crowd. Just the commander and task force members showed up. Where was Agent Walker and what was she and her FBI pal doing? The killer was incensed that she would not get her trophy picture. It was time to leave.

She walked down the roadway to her car, opened the driver's door and threw the camera case violently inside. The killer sat behind the steering wheel and pounded her fists in frustration. The white noise returned. It was just a buzz in the background, but it would grow to a pitch that would make her scream in agony, if she didn't do something to cage it.

Heading westbound on the 60, the killer's frustration mounted. She was trapped in the evening commuter traffic, and cars were bumper to bumper. The next exit was a mile and a half away. She would lose twenty minutes just getting to the off ramp. "The city streets will be busy, too. I should have thought of this!" the killer screamed out loud, as she mashed her hand on the horn like so many other angry commuters.

The killer began mumbling out loud as her car inched forward. "I'll go by the Tempe mosque and see what's going on, and then drive by 6 of 10's house just once, no stopping. Just make sure the heathens are safe at home. Safe…ha!" The killer laughed at their false sense of security. *By now they must have been told the killer had left, escaped, flew the coup!* She laughed her maniacal laugh again and savored the thoughts of what was coming their way later. *Don't forget, this car has to be torched and ditched,* she mentally reminded herself. The white noise increased as her rage grew, making it hard to concentrate. "Calm down, soldier. This is no way to act before battle." She grimly fought to regain control and enter military operations mode. "I'm on a mission for justice and revenge and can't lose sight of this again." Her mistakes had been mounting over the last few days. Stymied at every turn by that task force and Agent Walker, the killer hadn't figured out where they were getting their information. She'd left no clues to tie her or the military to her work.

The killer was struck with an idea. Pure inspiration. *How clever I am*, she thought. An opening to the off ramp approached, and the killer began looking for a place to park so she could make her phone call.

"As salaam'alaykum, Brother. Could I speak with Sister Jamilah? Tell her it's Sister Heather calling. I volunteered to help your wife with the transportation for the girl's youth group field trip next weekend. Thank you," she said and waited for the heathen's wife to come to the phone.

"Wa 'alaykum as salaam," the killer responded when the deceiver greeted her. "I went by Sister Zarinah's house, but no one seems to be at home, and I lost her phone number. I needed to ask her about the Qur'an class she teaches on Saturday."

The deceiver lowered her voice and replied, "Don't call Sis Zarinah right now. She is at the masjid and she's busy there, but I don't know what she is doing. There's something happening at the masjid. I don't know what, but my husband told me that we can't go there until further notice. We are supposed to go to the Phoenix masjid until the imam gives us the okay."

The killer's mind raced. She must not act too curious. Wouldn't do to question the woman, as she only knew what her husband told her. The killer lowered her voice to increase the sense of intimacy between her and the woman. "It must be something to do with those awful killings of our dear sisters. I have been so afraid, living alone as I do."

"There's some kind of meeting going on, but even my husband can't go to it. I overheard him tell Brother Fahd, Sister Fawzia's husband, that there are more armed security now. I don't understand. If we can't even *go* to the masjid, then why is there a need for more security?"

Not wanting to say much more as the deceiver's husband might ask her what the call was about, the killer said, "I'm sure everything is okay, and we'll know when it is the right time. I wouldn't be too concerned. Probably just extra security because of the increased vandalism. I have to go. Keep me in mind when the field trip gets rescheduled."

The killer sat and waited until the queasy feeling in her stomach subsided. The white noise ratcheted up to another level. She fought to control it. She popped the trunk button in the glove box, got out of the car, and retrieved her head scarf, gloves, and cloak from it. Looking around to see if anyone was on the street or in the yards and finding no one and with no traffic approaching in either direction, the killer quickly put on the clothes. She returned to the driver's seat, turned on the ignition and drove as quickly as possible in the direction of the Tempe mosque.

Thirty minutes later, she parked her car in the back parking lot behind the Phoenician restaurant, where she had a full view of the vehicles parked in the mosque parking lot across the street. The lights the Muslims had installed to help prevent theft and vandalism shone down on the vehicles parked close to the wall of the mosque.

The killer took the night vision goggles out of the shopping bag on the passenger seat and put them on. She took out her list of names with 6 of 10's name circled in red. Next to each name was the license plate number of the car driven by the male member of the family. The plate numbers on her list matched the plate numbers of five of the vehicles parked in the mosque parking lot. Six of 10's husband was at the secret meeting being held at the mosque. The killer took off the goggles and could hardly contain herself. An unexpected opportunity to salvage her mission!

Instead of going inside the restaurant, the killer started the car and drove with confidence and calm. She would complete the mission now before the task force could catch up with her and leave behind a cold and dead end trail. She would be long gone before they found 6 of 10 and her bratty heathen kids. The killer knew her window of opportunity was finite. The husband could leave the mosque anytime. She did not want any interruptions. He must find the bodies and wail in his sorrow. The words, "I'm coming for you 6 of 10," were repeated over and over in an evil monotone as the she made her way to the familiar neighborhood and home.

Catch Me If You Dare

Rainey was seated in front of the easel with a front face picture of Lieutenant Stewart in full military uniform pinned to the tablet she was working on. Rainey closed her eyes and concentrated on the face of the woman she had smiled at in the hardware store aisle and thought she saw her jogging one morning in the park and wearing the baseball cap. Rainey felt strongly that both women were the same person. *Call me, Sara.* If the woman had been wearing a wig, Sara would have noticed when they were in the hardware store. Sara had a thing about wigs. Rainey had sent her a text message reminding her of the woman.

Sara saw the Tempe police car with an officer standing next to the driver's door as the chopper landed in the ASU football field.

Lieutenant Jerald, the captain, and Sara stepped out of the chopper and hurried over to the waiting officer. "Officer Smith, Tempe Police Department. Ready to go?" the officer said, while opening the rear door for Sara.

"Evening, Officer. Straight to the Tempe mosque," replied Lieutenant Jerald for the group.

Sara took out her phone and dialed Zarinah's number. "Hello Zarinah. We are about five minutes away from the mosque. Meet us at the back door with the clothes and keys to the house and car. Okay?"

Sara closed the phone cover. "She's waiting now. I hope we get there before the killer does." Seven minutes later the team was in the intended victim's family car with Lieutenant Jerald driving and heading for the intended victim's home.

"When we get a couple of blocks from the house, the captain will get out and begin a perimeter search in case the killer's already there waiting for the family to return. When we drive up and park in the driveway, wait until I open the door for you, Sara. Don't forget you need to be holding a sleeping baby in your arms. You are a Muslim mama and not some bad ass FBI ace." The lieutenant's humor broke the tension and the officers grinned at each other.

"We're ready. As far as we know, the killer doesn't know about the captain. He's our ace," Sara said, as she adjusted the head scarf at her chin.

"If we arrive before she does, then she'll be the one getting a big surprise," the captain said. He cleared his throat. "I know she's killed one of your own, Jerald, and all those innocent women and one of our soldiers, Corporal Summers, but I'd like to try and take her alive…if only because of the memory of the officer, nurse, and human being she once was. She saved as many or more lives as she has taken. She'll never be free if we do take her in. I can guarantee that. She'll spend the rest of her life in a military prison." Daniels' voice was low and steady. Sara was certain he was sincere.

"If we can take her alive, fine. But if we can't, then I have no qualms about blowing her away," replied the lieutenant. Sara remained silent. What could she say that would not negatively tilt the uneasy truce between them?

Rainey's cell phone rang. "It's me. Ya doing okay, Rainey? Sara didn't wait for a response but plowed ahead…time was critical now. "Remember that woman you smiled at in the same aisle at that hardware store we stopped to get some stuff? She was wearing a wig. It was a high-end one that only someone who works with wigs or wears them would recognize. It was hand-made and was 100% human hair. Those wigs are designed special and cost a mint."

"When we passed each other in the aisle and I smiled at her, just for a moment she looked vaguely familiar, but then the thought escaped me. I could swear that she's the same woman I saw in the Cardinals baseball cap jogging in the park," Rainey replied.

"I'd say that was a coincidence but…" Sara and Rainey said together, "There are no coincidences in a police investigation!"

"The three of you watch your backs," Rainey said as their conversation ended.

The killer parked her car two streets south of 6 of 10's house. She grabbed the night vision goggles and her grocery bag filled with her tools. Dressed as a Muslim woman, she walked casually down the sidewalks, head bent, and eyes downcast. She didn't meet anyone. Most of the homes had their front room lights on, drapes closed, and a front porch light on where no car was parked in the carport or driveway. No garages in this neighborhood.

The killer looked at her wrist watch as she made her way to 6 of 10's street. It was almost 8:30. The sky was now pitch black. The moon, partially covered by low hanging clouds, was just a sliver in the sky and the stars were obscured by the haze of pollution hanging in the air.

The killer entered an alleyway, keeping close to the five foot block wall that separated properties from the alley. Her dark clothing blending in, she was a silent shadow that moved quickly until she came to the wall behind the house she would soon enter.

Over the wall with ease, and then crossing the small lawn that made up the back yard, the killer took off the goggles, putting them in the paper bag while taking out her tools. She remained silent listening for sounds of the children or 6 of 10 inside the house. Nothing. *She's probably putting the brats to bed. Maybe even sitting on the bed reading them a bedtime story.* The killer pictured the scene. She would come quietly to the doorway. Maybe one of the brats would see her first and say something. She'd look up to see the gun fire silencing her little darlings. She'd scream but there would be no one to hear her.

The killer shook her head as if to clear the mental images. Just minutes from now she wouldn't need to imagine anything.

It took less than a minute to pick the lock and enter through the back door. The kitchen was dark. She stood still listening. A growing unease gripped her. The house felt empty. *NO!* her mind shrieked. *She has to be here. She deserves to die.* The killer paused in the entryway to the great room. Silence greeted her. The killer's pulse began to race, and the white noise that had been simmering just below the surface started screaming. The killer grabbed the sides of her head as pain after searing pain rocked her. *Stop it. Calm down.* She had to get control of herself and the mission.

With extreme caution, the killer walked into every room and confirmed that the house was empty.

Drawers were opened with clothes falling out. Beds were unmade. The killer knew 6 of 10 and her family had left in a hurry.

The killer walked back to the living room and stared at the meager possessions this heathen family treasured. The prayer rugs rolled up and in a corner of the room. The bookshelves crammed with the sick words that fed their minds. The white noise was now a roar and the killer exploded in rage. She took out her knife and began slashing at everything. She turned over chairs, smashed anything that was breakable. She raced to each bedroom and destroyed everything. Still the rage boiled up from inside her. Her eyes were glazed, and she was breathing heavy—almost panting. Such was the physical energy she was using to destroy everything in the house. Dishes were smashed in the kitchen…cupboards kicked in. The killer left nothing untouched as she vented her fury. She lifted the sleeve of the cloak and cut her arm. She watched as her blood dripped into the cup. The killer bound her arm and then carried the half filled small cup of her own blood to the living room and wrote her message on the wall.

Shaking with rage, the killer realized that 6 of 10, her family, and all the families of the names on her list were in the mosque. It was now a fortress. She would never be able to get inside. Time had run out, and her mission here had failed. She had to move on. There would be other targets. She would find them. She would fulfill the mission, but not here and not now. *Escape!* The word cut through her thoughts. Yes. The word moved like shock waves. She didn't know how the cops had figured things out...it didn't matter. They had won this round. "I must get out of here and survive. The mission hadn't failed completely. I am alive and I'll hunt again," the killer spoke softly to the empty room, as she accepted this temporary defeat.

She grabbed her paper sack, tossed the bloody knife into it, and pulled out the .22 with the silencer. The cops could be on their way here right now. She panicked momentarily. They could be waiting for her outside. *Steady. You've been in tight spots before.* The killer's survival instincts and training kicked in as the white noise abated, and she made her way through the kitchen to the back door.

Lieutenant Jerald slowed the car as it approached the driveway. The living room light was turned off. The outside porch light was turned on, and the drapes were drawn as Zarinah had told them they would be. No one was outside and the street was empty save a few cars parked at the end of the street that they had already checked out and cleared.

"Ready, Sara?" the lieutenant said quietly, and looked over at his partner. She picked up the life-sized baby doll wrapped in the blanket and nodded her head. A small smile appeared momentarily and then disappeared. The lieutenant keyed his radio and spoke softly. "You ready, Captain?"

The captain answered, "The outer perimeter is clear. I'm at the backyard wall. I'm going over the wall, and I'll look at the back of the house and call you back. Sit tight."

Lieutenant Jerald came back and said, "Captain hold your position. I said hold your position. Do not. Do not go over that wall. Hold your position." The lieutenant and Sara waited tensely for the captain to respond.

The killer had just passed through the back door when she saw a dark shadow coming over the wall. She didn't hesitate. She aimed at the shadow as it cleared the wall and started to stand. The shadow was facing her when she fired twice. She thought she heard the words "Lieutenant Stewart" just before the dark shadow went down. The killer quickly, but cautiously, approached the shadow lying on the ground next to the wall. There wasn't any movement. She heard a voice coming from a radio. It was on the shadow. The shadow was a man—a cop—not a shadow. Now it was nothing but a body. The killer went over the wall without even glancing down at the man she had shot. As she came to the end of the alleyway and turned the corner heading south on the sidewalk she heard someone shouting behind her. Then sirens began to wail. The killer didn't stop running or look back.

Lieutenant Jerald waited thirty seconds and called the captain. No response. "Let's go. Something is wrong, Sara."

Sara tried to raise the captain, but he didn't answer. She tossed the baby doll into the back seat, ripped the head scarf off her head and tore frantically at the cloak she was wearing as she opened the passenger door.

Lieutenant Jerald called the task force team just outside the outer perimeter to close in fast and quiet and use extreme caution.

"Sara, we both go in the front together. I take lead," he said. Sara nodded. Her weapon was drawn and she and the lieutenant approached the front door. They paused and listened. Nothing. No sounds could be heard from inside.

Slowly the lieutenant tried the front door. It was locked. He inserted the key, turned it, and both he and Sara stood to either side of the doorway as the door was eased open with the lieutenant's right foot.

They stood momentarily in shock at the bloody message written on the wall. They had no time to linger. Sara sucked in her breath, and she and the lieutenant did a room to room search, all the time making calls to the captain, who remained unresponsive. When they got to the kitchen, they saw the back door was open. The lieutenant and Sara carefully eased through the doorway and began scanning the back yard.

"He's down!" Sara yelled, as she dashed across the yard and went down next to Daniels' body.

"Officer down! Officer down!" Lieutenant Jerald yelled into his radio. "Get an ambulance rolling now."

Lieutenant Jerald bent down next to Sara, who was crying silent tears. The Captain's head was cradled in her lap.

The lieutenant ran back through the house and out the front door and stood on the porch barking orders. "Get me the crime scene unit here now. I need three squads ASAP for a grid perimeter search. We don't have any time to lose."

Phoenix radio answered in the affirmative. The task force officers came running up the driveway and stopped in front of their commander. "That psycho shot the Captain. Agent James is with him in the back yard. Looks like the killer got the captain coming over the wall into the yard. She was already here." He told them to spread out and look for a female on foot wearing Muslim or street clothes. "Stop and detain any female and use extreme caution. She could be the killer and she is armed with a knife and a semi-auto and silencer. Detective Harris. I want you to stay in front of this door and no one…I mean no one is to enter the house until the crime scene unit arrives and don't let them in until I am back here. I am locking the door," the lieutenant said, as he opened it and went through, closing it behind him.

The lieutenant stood very still and stared hard at the wall. The killer's message was written boldly in huge letters, block printed in the killer's unique style.

He knew that his team was here while the killer was inside, but he was just minutes too late. That psycho was gone, leaving destruction and a message behind. He had a phone call to make to Sara's partner. It was a hard thing he had to tell her. One last time he looked at the wall before heading out the back door to where Sara was waiting with the fallen officer.

Agent Walker. Catch me if you dare. SK

Epilogue

Rainey and Sara sat in a corner of the hospital waiting room away from all the task force members milling around holding Styrofoam cups of bitter coffee and talking in hushed voices. Captain Daniels was taken into surgery three hours ago. His chances of making it through surgery grew slimmer with each minute that passed.

"You look beat, Sara. Why don't you go back to the house, take a shower and get some fresh clothes…take a nap? I'll call you if anything changes here."

Sara nodded and gave Rainey a quick hug. "You're right. I need to get out of these clothes." Sara's pants and shirt were caked with Captain Daniels' blood. The blood had dried and felt stiff against Sara's skin. "You'll call me if there is any change at all?"

"You know I will. Take my car and get out of here," Rainey said, handing over the car keys.

Rainey hadn't meant to fall asleep but the gentle shake to her shoulder roused her awake. "What's happened? Is it Captain Daniels? Is he okay?"

Rainey looked at the sorrow and pain etched in the weary lines of Lieutenant Jerald's face. He sat down next to Rainey and covered both her cold hands in his own. "It's about Sara."

"No! No!" Rainey screamed and jerked her hands away and

covered her ears. She didn't want to hear what the lieutenant was going to tell her.

Lieutenant Jerald gently took her hands again in his own and said, "Rainey I don't know any other way to tell you this but just give it to you straight. Sara got to your house, opened the front door, and a bomb SK planted exploded. I'm so sorry, Rainey but Sara is gone." Rainey went limp. Lieutenant Jerald caught her before she could hit the floor.

Rainey hurried across the parking lot, head down, looking in her purse for her car keys. It had been a year since she lost her best friend and home in Arizona. She was back teaching at NYU.

The briefcase bulging with her students' final exams slipped from under her arm and fell to the pavement. "Damn!"

"Looks like you could use a hand."

Rainey knew that voice. Her eyes traveled up the length of his long legs and came to rest on the face of Captain Daniels.

"What do you want?" Rainey's harsh words tore at him. His mega-watt smile disappeared as Rainey stared hard at him. Only the remnants of past pain and what? pity? looked back at her.

So softly spoken that Rainey had to lean forward to hear his words, "SK is on the hunt. I need your help."

About the Author

L. D. Alan retired as a Sergeant in 2000 after a twenty-six year career in law enforcement. The author lives in the Southwest USA and enjoys writing and spending time with family and friends. *Catch Me If You Dare* is the first book in a planned book series. *Gotcha!* is the second book in the series. Look for it in late 2010.

Gotcha!

After a year in hiding, the Scarf Killer surfaces again in sunny California and Rainey is pulled back into the massive manhunt when the killer strikes out at victim '6 of 10'. Rainey knows that the body count will rise unless this murderous psychopath is stopped permanently.

Don't miss the second book in the Rainey Walker series, *Gotcha!*, available in the Fall of 2010.

Visit L. D. Alan's blog at:
www.raineywalkerseries.wordpress.com

Breinigsville, PA USA
21 June 2010
240248BV00001B/6/P